MW00478030

SEASONS OF CHANGE

ELIZABETH JOHNS

Copyright © Elizabeth Johns, 2014
All rights reserved
Cover Design by Wilette Youkey
Edited by Tessa Shapcott
Historical Content Heather King

ISBN-13 978-1503069510
ISBN-10 150369516
No part of this publication may be reproduced, stored, copied, or transmitted without
the prior written permission of the copyright owner.

This is a work of fiction. Names, characters, places, and incidents either are the product
of the author's imagination or are used fictitiously. Any resemblance to actual persons,
living or dead, business establishments, events, or locales is entirely coincidental.

PROLOGUE

This was war. Beatrice was the look-out, and her cousin Elinor perched in the tree, watching and waiting. They would have revenge—even if Beatrice was too missish to climb the tree as she was frequently told. But what the boys had done was unforgivable. Flour buckets booby-trapped over doorways, short-folding their sheets, and even frogs and fish in their beds were forgivable. Spiders and snakes were not. She would have nightmares for years as a result of that prank.

The trap had taken the girls two hours to set, and many more to prepare. The gamekeeper had not asked why Beatrice needed a net and a rope, thank goodness. It had better work. She could not stand the mortification if she failed. She was just as good as Elinor. She would prove it. Even though the cousins were of similar age, they were not of similar tastes or disposition. Elinor was an outgoing tomboy whom everyone adored. Beatrice was an introvert, and was averse to most things outdoors. Especially horses, much to the dismay of her father. The horse-mad Duke was constantly trying to urge Beatrice to be brave like her cousin. She preferred her dolls and books, thank you. However, there was nothing quite like revenge against a common enemy to pull Beatrice and Elinor together.

After waiting patiently for what felt like an eternity, the four boys came in to view, and Beatrice signalled to Elinor. Closer, closer, now! Elinor released the net, and they watched the boys struggle to free themselves. Then Beatrice mercilessly pulled on the rope to tip over the pots of smelly slop that Cook had concocted (being deathly afraid of spiders herself). They ran as fast as their nine-year-old feet would carry them, giggling all the way.

They made it back to the house, up to the nursery and closed the door and turned the lock. Now Beatrice could breathe. "Did you think it worked all right?" she asked, hoping for approval.

"Yes! It worked perfectly." Elinor managed, though gasping for air. And that led to more and more giggles. "What do you think they will do next?"

"I have no idea, but we best be ready," Beatrice said through her laughter.

That evening, Beatrice peeked into the large room in the nursery where the children took their dinner together. The coast was clear. She had no desire to face any of the boys alone. Hopefully one of the servants would appear with the food before the boys did. Then she smelled the stench, and turned to see to whom it belonged.

"That was clever." Rhys paused and leaned against the door. "For a nine-year-old girl." She tried not to preen. No one ever praised her, only Elinor.

Trying to cover her nose, Beatrice eyed him sceptically, not sure if that was a compliment or not. Rhys Godfrey, the heir to Earl Vernon, was a distant cousin and friend that Andrew Abbott, her first cousin, and Nathaniel, Lord Fairmont, her brother, had brought home from Eton for part of the summer holiday. "Elinor and Cook helped. Are you declaring a truce?"

He shrugged. "I suppose. I wanted to warn you to check your bed tonight," he whispered to her, looking around to make sure he was not caught tattling by the other boys.

"I have learned my lesson, but I appreciate the warning."

Rhys leaned over and kissed Beatrice on the cheek.

"Goodbye." He winked and threw a big smile at her.

Beatrice narrowed her eyes. He smiled and ran off to find his fellow conspirators, and—she hoped—to bathe. Beatrice stood and watched after him in awe, touching her cheek where he had kissed her.

"Goodbye, Rhys," she whispered after him. He was actually *nice* to her. She wondered how long it would last. No one ever seemed to like her for long.

CHAPTER 1

1815, ELEVEN YEARS LATER...

*L*ady Beatrice was determined to exact her revenge tonight at the tenants' ball. She was disgusted with her loose cousin, Elinor, coming back from America and stealing all of her attention. She had never been good enough for her father since Nathaniel left, and she had always been compared to the infallible Elinor. She let her maid, Jenny, place the finishing touches to her coiffure as she preened in front of the looking glass. She thought the unadorned, flowing white satin gown perfect for emphasizing her purity tonight. Beatrice would never be described as angelic, but this would do.

"Lovely as always, milady. I just hope his Grace does not see you." Jenny said worriedly as she fastened the diamond necklace on her mistress. Beatrice shook her head at the diamonds; it would ruin the effect. Jenny replaced the diamonds and selected the pearls instead. Beatrice had been forbidden to leave her room during the ball after her father had banished her to the country. Once her plan was carried out, she would return to her room with the Duke none the wiser.

"Do not worry yourself, Jenny. I can manage him. The Duke is stern on the outside but soft on the inside." Beatrice smiled with satisfaction as she checked the finished product. Satisfied, she turned toward the door. "I am going to enjoy myself very much." She gave a malicious smile and went out of the door.

"Wait, milady!" Jenny called after her.

Beatrice looked over her shoulder. "Yes?"

"Do you want me to make sure no one is about?"

"That is what footmen are for." She waved Jenny off with her hand and kept moving, anticipation in every step. Beatrice had spread a story about her cousin, Elinor Abbott, at Elinor's coming-out ball. She had intended the story to send her cousin crying back to America, but instead she caused a betrothal between Elinor and Lord Easton.

Beatrice's father, the Duke of Loring, had overheard her telling the story of Easton and Elinor being unaccompanied on the voyage from America, and he had the gall to punish Beatrice for spreading gossip! He had actually banished her to remain in the country for the next season with no pin money. She laughed maliciously. See if that would keep her away! She was not about to sit by idly in the country while Elinor reaped all of her rewards.

Beatrice slipped into the ballroom through a side door. She spotted her father and went in the opposite direction, stalking her prey. How perfect; Elinor was talking to Nathaniel. Beatrice had recently found out that Nathaniel had taken Elinor's innocence. She could hardly wait to send her packing on the next ship out of England. The valiant Lord Easton would never want her once he found out she was not the pure, innocent virgin he thought she was. No one would be able to save Elinor from this.

Beatrice sauntered over to Lord Easton and approached from the side as he watched Elinor with Nathaniel. "They will always have a special bond, you know. I wonder if they still have feelings for each other after all these years? Perhaps Father is right that they should wed."

Easton gave an unworried shrug.

"Come, let us dance and take your mind off her. It is not gentlemanly to brood," Beatrice cooed as she pulled Easton toward the dance floor. Easton did not take his eyes from Elinor as Nathaniel began to waltz with her. Noticing Easton's gaze, Beatrice continued her plot as they made their way across the floor toward the pair. "You must admit they make a charming couple." And now for the final thrust. "I suppose I would still pine for the person I gave my innocence to as well," she said rather loudly, just as Elinor and Nathaniel brushed up against them. She could not have timed it better if she had tried.

Easton furiously stormed off the dance floor. Elinor stood there stunned and stared at her. Beatrice fought back a smile. She could not manage a look of innocence. They stared each other down; the standoff ended when Elinor turned, ran off the dance floor and straight out of the terrace doors.

As Beatrice watched Elinor and her betrothed flee in opposite directions, she felt rather pleased that her plan had come to fruition effortlessly. Until she felt a large hand grab her and spin her around. Her brother stood over her, eyes blazing with fury. She then noticed the music had stopped, and the crowd stood still watching her every move. Drat!

Nathaniel hissed through clenched teeth, "Smile and walk off the floor with me before Father throws you over his shoulder."

Beatrice glared, but walked with him, her head held high. She was not going to cower away with her tail between her legs. Nathaniel led her into the library and shut the door behind them. He crossed his arms over his chest and glared at her without a word. She refused to back down. "Well?"

"Do you care to explain yourself, Bea?" he asked calmly. "You'd better come up with an explanation before Father finds out and wrings your neck."

"I did nothing wrong." She crossed her arms over her chest and held her head high.

"Nothing wrong? You think this is all about you? I am beyond disgusted. I do not know what happened to you while I was away, but I am ashamed to call you my sister right now."

"Well, that is the pot calling the kettle black. You have no right to judge me!" She threw up her hands haughtily. A Duke's heir could get away with murder, and she was being reprimanded for this?

7

"I understand how you feel, but I know of what I speak. You are heading down the same path I did. In fact, I might recommend Father implement the same treatment for you." Nathaniel began to pace the floor in front of the fire.

"As if I could join the army." Beatrice walked over and laughed in his face. "Do you think you are protecting your beloved? She has eyes only for Easton, you idiot!"

He stopped and towered over her. "You have no idea, do you?" He placed his hands on her shoulders and looked her in the eye. He hesitated then said quietly, "Bea, I violated Elly."

"Do not be ridiculous!" Beatrice retorted.

"I am in earnest, Bea," Nathaniel said sombrely.

Beatrice stood there as if she had been slapped, too stunned for words. "V-violated?" She slumped down into the chair behind her, and her face fell into her hands. "Oh God, what have I done?" She had wanted to put Elinor back in her place when she thought her loose and pretending to be something she was not.

"You cannot toy with people like they are game pieces, Bea. What changed you into this malicious scheming shrew while I was gone? I want to keep anyone from hurting her more. That is the least I can do."

She shook her head. That angered her. She did not try to suppress the indignation building within. "Pray, do not imagine to understand how it was for me when you left!" She stood and marched toward the windows then spun around back to face him. "Father has never recovered from having to send you away. I was never a substitute for you. Then, he wanted me to be like her! He paid no attention to me, and I was left with Mother."

He scoffed. "Like mother, like daughter." He shook his head. "Bea, you cannot use Mother as an excuse. You and I have both wronged Elinor, and I plan to spend the rest of my life trying to make it up to her."

She still did not speak. He sighed. "You'd best consider what to say to Father. At this point, you will be fortunate if he does not send you to a convent."

A booming voice resounded from the doorway, "I think a convent is an excellent idea."

The Duke entered the room calmly and sat in his chair behind the desk. He was eerily silent. He was never silent. He stared at Beatrice for what felt like eternity, and then finally spoke.

"Beatrice, you had best go to your room. We will discuss this in the morning."

She stood there, shocked into silence for a moment, unable to believe what she had heard. Never before had he dismissed her without a lecture. Too afraid to protest, she meekly obeyed without further eye contact.

Nathaniel closed the door behind Beatrice and waited to see if his father wished for his presence or not. The Duke looked up and waved him into a chair.

"Do you think a convent will make any difference?" The Duke looked as miserable as he felt. He did not even have to ask Nathaniel what Beatrice had done. "I still cannot fathom how you managed to become so disguised that you forced yourself upon Elly in the first place. And now your sister is so demented she thinks to ruin Elly further," the Duke said as he continued staring into the fire.

"The army managed to reform me. I think Bea must feel true pain in order to have a chance at seeing what she has done and surmise there is a world beyond herself." Nathaniel knew this from personal experience.

"Pray tell, where did I go wrong? You have had the best of everything, and this is the thanks I receive in return." He shook his head in dismay. "If you were not the only heir, I would send you back. I still cannot believe I urged her to marry you." That was as near as the Duke ever came to admitting he was wrong.

"I will work the rest of my days to be worthy of her forgiveness. No one regrets what happened more than I. I can never take away what I did, and I have to live with that," Nathaniel said quietly.

9

The Duke looked back at him with pain in his eyes. There was a soft knock at the door, and the Duke waved Nathaniel over to answer, too distraught to speak. Lord Vernon followed him back into the room.

"Your Grace." Vernon made a quick bow.

"I suppose you do not want Beatrice any more, either. Cannot say that I blame you." The Duke sighed loudly. "Nathaniel thinks we should send her to a convent," he said resignedly, looking to Vernon to give his opinion.

Nothing could have astonished Vernon more than the thought of Beatrice in a convent. They sat in silence a few moments, then Lord Vernon looked up. "Perhaps there is another way. It is just shy of a convent, but Easton has convinced me to start another orphanage up at my Scottish property. I use it as a hunting box mostly, but it is well enough. Perhaps she could help out there. See the less fortunate and all that."

Nathaniel laughed mockingly. "How would we keep her there? She would be on the first equipage that drove by."

"No chance of that. The place is so remote you cannot find it unless you know it is there. Even Bea would not dare run away from there, especially in the winter. And my spinster aunt Mary lives there. She can look after her."

"Do you honestly think it would work?" The Duke looked sceptical.

"We have to hope there is still a shred of decency left." Vernon walked over and stared into the fire.

"She has no choice but to understand the delicacy of her situation. She has already defied me once. I will not condone this behaviour any longer," the Duke said, clearly out of patience.

"I must say she seemed shocked when I told her the truth of what happened," Nathaniel interjected in Beatrice's defence.

"May I speak to her before she goes?" Vernon asked the Duke.

"Are you sure you wish to do that, Vernon?" the Duke asked, surprised.

"Considering I have been planning to marry her since the nursery, I think I should at least say goodbye," Vernon pointed out.

"Very well. I am going to inform her of her fate in the morning. You may see her then," the Duke consented.

Beatrice walked to her room in shock. If she could reverse the last few hours—no months—she would. Why had no one ever told her what happened? Elly had been violated? By Nathaniel? Beatrice could not believe her brother capable of such an atrocity, even though he had certainly sown his wild oats before going into the army. So many things began to fall into place when she thought back. Beatrice felt ill to the core of her being, suffered pangs of conscience she had thought long gone. A tear of remorse fell down her cheek. She knew her father would send her to a convent. She had never seen him so angry, so quiet. She had no idea what would become of her there, or what she would be expected to do.

Even though Beatrice knew she had done Elly an injustice, it was still hard to swallow her pride. When she thought about what Nathaniel had done, the offences were incomparable and it brought back all of the old hurts from her childhood. She determined she would take whatever punishment her father doled out and not flinch. If she was on her best behaviour, she would be able to come back soon. She would prove them wrong. She would.

The next morning, the dreaded talk with her father arrived. Beatrice had just received the summons. She had barely managed to sleep at all, knowing she had been awful, but not knowing what to do to make things right. There were some things that could not be forgotten. She glanced in the looking glass and saw dark circles and red, swollen eyes. Jenny helped her into a dress and pulled her hair back without so much as a word or look in the eye. She walked slowly through the house with an impending sense of doom.

Beatrice knocked on the door to the library, and then entered quietly at her father's command. She stood alone before him, her mother noticeably absent.

"Sit." He was still eerily quiet. She did as she was ordered.

The Duke looked as if he had been up all night, but he had taken the time to change clothes and shave. "I only have one question. What inspired this change of heart in you?" He looked long and hard at her, searching for the answer. She remained silent. What good would it do to answer anyway?

After several minutes of silence, the Duke stood and walked over to the window. When he finally spoke, he did so quietly without looking at her. "First, you will write and apologize to Elinor. I will not force her to suffer your presence." Beatrice looked up in surprise, though she should not have been. "Secondly, you will release Lord Vernon from your betrothal. He deserves better." Beatrice looked away trying to hide the tears. This was worse than she had ever imagined it would be, and she could tell he was not finished yet. "Thirdly, you will leave all of your possessions, save two dresses. I recommend something warm since it gets quite cold where you are going." She felt a deep sense of foreboding when he uttered those words. "Lastly, Lord Vernon has asked to speak with you, though I cannot pretend to know why. The carriage will be ready to leave in one hour." He walked out of the door without a look backwards, never asking for her side of the story, assuming the worst.

She sat in stunned silence. Though she should have expected nothing less. He never had affection for her like he did for her cousin and brother. At least she had held her tongue. She would not humiliate herself further. She looked up and Rhys, Lord Vernon, stood there before her. He looked hurt, disappointed. She dropped her eyes to her hands, unable to meet his gaze.

"Why, Bea?" he asked so quietly she could barely hear him.

She shook her head but did not look up. She did not want him to see the tears. She could not bring herself to admit to him that she was jealous.

"I have lost my best friend, my love. Does she still exist? Or is it only in my imagination?" he asked with anguish.

She could not speak for the lump in her throat and trying to hold back sobs. He took her silence as her answer.

"Very well," he said curtly. "This is goodbye then." He turned on his heel and walked away from her.

Beatrice found herself standing alone in the entry hall holding only a small portmanteau, not remembering the past hour of her life. The butler stood there devoid of emotion, but no one had come to tell her goodbye. What did she expect? Her father had as good as cast her out. She took a deep breath and headed for the door. She was no coward. She would face this and hope her father would welcome her back as he had Nathaniel. She was not ruined, and she had not raped anyone, after all. She cringed to herself, feeling guilty. She had been playing a game with Elinor, assuming the worst, never fathoming the truth.

"Bea."

She turned at the sound of his voice and found her brother standing there looking empathetic. She had a hard time looking him in the eye after what he had told her he had done to Elinor.

"Yes?"

"Father asked me to give you this." He handed her a small purse and a note. He looked at her with pity.

"So, this is it then," she said resignedly. "I thought Mother would at least bother to say farewell, but I assume she is in bed with the vapours."

Nathaniel nodded. "She dare not argue with Father but is rather vexed with him."

"She is only vexed about the gossip my absence will cause."

"At least you do not have to begin with breaking yourself of an opium and whisky habit." He laughed harshly, clearly remembering his own forced exile from the family. "It will pass quickly. Just be agreeable, and Father will allow you to return soon. He has eyes and ears everywhere. I still do not know how he knows, but he does." Nathaniel pulled her into an awkward embrace, and she pulled away, unused to affection, and not sure she wanted it from him. She walked out of the door and into the waiting carriage and refused to look back.

CHAPTER 2

*R*hys, Lord Vernon, walked in shock towards the stables, talking himself out of turning around at least ten times, mounted his horse, and rode at breakneck speed with no destination in mind. He eventually found himself riding toward London, only stopping at the Dog and Fox Inn for a fresh horse and a bottle of their finest whisky. His heart felt like it had been ripped from his chest, beaten to a pulp, and then shoved back in barely beating. How had things come to this? He had loved Beatrice from the day he first saw her eleven years ago. He always knew he would marry her, even though their fathers had later formalized the arrangement. They often jested about it, but Rhys would never have forced Beatrice to marry him without her consent. He was one of the few who rejoiced at his arranged marriage.

Rhys had finally tired of waiting for Beatrice to reciprocate his feelings, so he had tried to prompt her into showing some sign that she cared for him—in more than a brotherly way—by flirting with Elinor. But all that seemed to accomplish was turning her into a shrew. Or was she vulgar all along, and had he been too blind to notice her imperfections? He was sure she was not like that before her entrée to the *haut ton*, before her mother and her ilk got their claws into her, and before Nathaniel left. He had foolishly expected her to apologize and leave with him. He never anticipated blatant rejection. He shook his head out of his reverie and took another long swig from the bottle.

Why not be a bawdy house song come to life? he pondered as he belched. What had saving himself for Beatrice achieved? She obviously did not hold the same level of affection as he. It was too late for remonstrance. She had made her choice clear: she preferred exile to him. He took another swig and wiped the dribble away with his sleeve.

"Is my spinster aunt Mary a preferable choice to me?" He tried conversing with his horse. The horse snorted in reply. "I do not think so, either."

Was he just supposed to walk away and get on with his life as if Beatrice was not a significant part of it? He shook his head. No. "Without so much as a by your leave."

He would allow himself a mourning period of sorts, and then continue with his life. He needed a wife to have an heir, and he would make a decision based on logic. His heart belonged to one person, and she had toyed with it like a cat with a mouse. No more.

By the time Rhys made it back to London, the bottle was long gone, the horse was winded and he was numb to all feeling, including the freezing temperatures. He dismounted at his stables and gave the horse to a groom, but kept walking past the house, not ready to confront reality. He found himself wandering the streets in the dark, with nary a care if he was a prime target for thieves or pickpockets. He could not bring himself to care about anything but erasing the agony he felt and the cause of it.

His head pounding and the world spinning, Rhys meandered into the theatre district. He resolved to banish his principles and drown his sorrows in whisky and women. It seemed to work for others in his class, just like marriages of convenience. He shuddered with distaste. He had never had to consider a loveless relationship before. Perhaps it would be acceptable to *like* the person he married. He could not imagine sitting across the table every day for the rest of his life with someone he did not even esteem. Beatrice had always understood him. She even understood his absurd humour. He sighed. He must divert his thoughts elsewhere.

Rhys strolled past the theatre trying to find someone who would tempt him, but he felt nothing but repulsion at every female who propositioned him. He could not even be tempted to partake of the most popular courtesan in town when she approached. Beatrice's face kept flashing before him, and the longing in his heart only seemed to worsen the longer he looked. He turned on his heel and walked away. He thrust his hands into his hair. What was the matter with him? Why could he not be like other men? He turned in the direction of his home and started to walk aimlessly. Perhaps more whisky would do the trick, but his aching head and churning stomach did not seem to agree.

He struggled up the steps into his town home, past his butler into his study and stumbled into the chair by the fire. He was becoming a maudlin drunk; he wanted nothing more than to weep. He was not prone to such emotions. Everywhere he looked he saw something that reminded him of her. He glanced at the picture hanging over the mantel that she had painted for him for his twenty-first birthday. It was a horrid painting, but he loved it, nevertheless. He stumbled out of his chair to his desk and rummaged through the drawers until he found the stack of letters she had written to him over the years. Each was tied with a dainty ribbon and smelled of lavender, her favourite scent. He took a deep sniff of the parchment and sat down in the chair and began to cry with his head in his hands.

He felt ridiculous; Beatrice would tell him he was being ridiculous were she here. He looked up through his fingers and saw the miniature of Beatrice on his desk. Her hazel eyes stared back at him.

"Must you mock me?" He thrust the portrait face down. He went back over to the decanter and poured another whisky, but could not drink it. He sat back down by the fire, letters in one hand, drink in the other, and stared at the flames, hoping they would provide some comfort.

~

Beatrice climbed into the carriage. Her father did not think she needed a chaperone or a maid where she was going. She had been dressed in her maid's dress, so she would not be confused as to her new station in life. She fiddled with the letter and purse her father had sent with her. She could not bring herself to open either one. What value had her father placed on her journey north? Was the letter for her, or for the person she was to be meeting from the convent?

Beatrice set the items aside. She would have more than ample time to ponder them on her journey. She was more heartbroken at the loss of Rhys than anything else at the moment. She felt like she could tolerate anything else but that. She had taken for granted that he would always be there. He always had been, even when she was all arms and legs and big eyes. She thought they would have been married by now, but Rhys had distanced himself the last few months as if waiting for something. She had done everything her mother had instructed—flirting with others, acting coy, feigning indifference—to no avail. Despite the arrangement their fathers had made, they both had to agree as adults. Rhys had still not proposed.

When Elinor had arrived, and he began to flirt with her, Beatrice had come undone inside. He was supposed to do that with her and *only her*. It had always been only her. Then she had overheard her grandmother talking about Elinor being ruined, and the seed of hate began to grow within her until the weed overtook the garden. Her mother and Lady Lydia seemed to revel in the gossip, and she had enjoyed the thought of making Elly suffer as she did.

A bump jostled her out of her reflections, and if she were honest, she knew she deserved to be reprimanded. She even felt guilty. But to be thrown out of the house and sent to a convent hundreds of miles away? She had to think the punishment did not fit the crime. She had done nothing out of the ordinary in society, and was encouraged by her mother. Her brother had been welcomed back like the proverbial prodigal son that the vicar would preach about, fatted calf and all. She was not going to give them the satisfaction of seeing her grovel or whine. She hardened her resolve and was determined to prove to everyone she was not the hateful, scheming, heartless Jezebel they all thought her.

The carriage pulled to an abrupt stop. The footman pulled open the door, handed her out, and then dropped her portmanteau at her feet. He then proceeded to jump back up onto the carriage that pulled away promptly. She watched the carriage roll down the lane, stunned. She looked around her trying to determine where she was. Perhaps it was time to open the letter and see.

Beatrice never imagined her father would have her deposited at a posting inn, but it appeared that was exactly what had occurred. This went against every tenet of propriety and behaviour that had been borne upon her; she could not reconcile it, regardless of her crimes. She heard someone yell for her to move away, and she barely missed being trampled by a coach, but not being splashed by mud. She shrieked and began to yell, then quickly realized she was the object of unkindly stares. She was no longer a Duke's daughter or a fine lady. She was dressed as a lady's maid or governess at best. Beatrice had never felt so invisible in her life. She shivered in the freezing temperatures, colder than ever since she was wet. Her shoulders sagged, and she made her way toward the inn to find a warm place to read the letter from her father, hoping he'd left her some direction. She could imagine him thinking it a valuable lesson for her to make her own way; this served to strengthen her resolve to prove him mistaken.

She strode purposefully in the door and looked around for someone to help her. She had only been in such a place once in her life, and they had been ushered into a private parlour immediately away from the commoners.

"Excuse me. Does anyone work here?" she called out to no one in particular.

None paid her any mind, save leers from some lecherous-looking men. Was there no one who would help her? She scanned the room again, trying not to make eye contact and spied a small table available on the side of the room. She walked tentatively toward the table, lugging her portmanteau, and sat down. She took a deep breath, then pulled out the letter. It was written by her father's secretary, of course. Disappointed, she read:

Dear Lady Beatrice,

I took the liberty of providing some direction for you on your journey. Your father provided the purse and address. He only allowed you ten pounds for your journey, so you must practice economy. You may purchase a ticket from there for the stagecoach that will take you to London, where you can take the mail-coach straight through to Dumfries in Scotland. A letter has been sent forth already to inform your host of your arrival. Hopefully, there will be someone to meet you there. If not, I would enquire about transport when you arrive to the enclosed address.

Your obedient servant,

Henry Foster

Beatrice sat there, terrified, hands shaking. Scotland? And she was to travel on the stagecoach? She had heard nothing but horrors about travelling in such a way. The closest she had come was taking a hack in London, and there had never been anyone she did not know in there with her. She had never even been allowed in public without a servant accompanying her. She swallowed an unladylike gulp and tried to gather her wits about her. How did one purchase a ticket? She had never paid for anything in her life. What exactly was economizing? It sounded extremely unpleasant, whatever it was.

She glanced around the room and finally saw a man who looked as if he worked there. She nervously approached the man.

"Pardon me, sir. Would you be able to tell me where I might purchase a ticket for the...the stage?"

The man eyed her up and down, raising a sceptical eyebrow at her. Were she dressed as her normal self she would have given him a set-down for the impertinence. Her plain cambric muslin did not seem to impress him.

"Fallen down the ladder, have ye?" he said with an amused snaggle-toothed grin.

It took every ounce of restraint in her being not to stomp her foot. She remained silent. He finally took pity on her. "Over there." He pointed his head in the other direction. "But ye better hurry or ye will miss the last one fer the day."

Beatrice hastily made her way to purchase her ticket as she heard a loud horn blow. Most of the people who had been sitting in the inn made their way outdoors, scrambling to get into the approaching coach. She followed them out and watched as trunk after trunk and person after person were loaded into and onto the vehicle. She was going to be sick.

"Are ye comin' or not, miss?" the coachman yelled to her. Her feet were glued to the ground as reality began to hit in full force. She nodded reluctantly and handed her bag to the man to be stowed with the others. Then she climbed into the coach, squeezed herself into the only remaining space and began to cry.

Nathaniel walked in to his father's study after seeing Beatrice off. The Duke stared with solemnity into the empty space. Nathaniel did not bother to greet him. What was there to say anyway? The Duke's secretary excused himself. In all likelihood, he did not want to have to witness any further drama from the family today. Wise man. The Duchess still had not left her room since she heard the Duke was sending her beloved Beatrice away.

Nathaniel thought the trip would be beneficial for Beatrice. The sister he'd left behind six years ago was not hateful and malicious. He suspected her behaviour was encouraged by his mother and not previously noted by his father. Nathaniel thought that once Beatrice saw life beyond the *ton*, it would open her eyes to what mattered. That was certainly the effect it had had on him.

"Nathaniel, thank God you are here. Please talk some sense into your father! Tell him to retrieve her at once!" the Duchess pronounced as she marched into the room.

"I suggested he send her away," Nathaniel said calmly.

That brought on a new round of hysterics and the Duchess swooned onto the floor. Nathaniel walked over and picked her up and placed her on the settee. Barnes walked in with the smelling salts as if on cue.

"You have been away too long if you thought your mother could tolerate a reasonable discussion," the Duke said as he observed the drama from his chair.

"Perhaps rusticating in Scotland would be beneficial to her as well," Nathaniel said dryly.

"Ungrateful wretch! How dare you speak of your poor mother's nerves in that manner." The Duchess lifted her head and chastised her son. Nathaniel's lips quivered. "Your father has ruined your sister by sending her away! Now everyone will wonder what she has done to be jilted. *Jilted!*" She threw her head back on the pillow.

"Vernon will not let them believe he jilted her. But let them wonder if she comes back reformed, Mother. She has the luxury of being the daughter of a Duke. The *ton* will look to you for guidance. If you act as though nothing occurred, I dare say they will also," Nathaniel reasoned with her on her own terms.

This pacified the Duchess somewhat, for she could not argue with her son's logic. She knew the *ton*'s ways better than anyone; it was what she lived for. "But without her maid!" she continued to argue.

"I am having her followed to ensure she makes it to Vernon's safely. I imagine by now she has already learned several valuable lessons from travelling alone. No one will know who she is. I daresay, even Beatrice knows better than to advertise that fact." The Duke was growing annoyed at being questioned.

"I still think it a wretched thing to do. She did nothing wrong as far as I am concerned." The Duchess put her nose in the air.

"I assure you, your concerns are ignorant. Pray, don't imagine I hold her at less fault than yourself. I know what I am about, Wilhelmina. This discussion is finished."

This set-down was met with an indignant, "Well!" before the Duchess returned to the sanctum of her apartments to be consoled by her vinaigrette and hartshorn.

CHAPTER 3

*R*hys sat in his study unshaven, hung over and staring at the same wall of books he had for the past week. Whisky did not seem to be solving his problems. Not that he had any expectations in that quarter. He vaguely heard a knock on the door and voices in the entry hall, but he was too blue-devilled to be home to visitors.

He knew in his mind that he could not stay in this room forever avoiding the future. He knew he should eat and sleep. But his heart was not ready to move on, to act like Beatrice had never existed.

"Vernon?" No response. "Vernon! What has got you in such a pucker?" Rhys continued to stare at the wall. All he offered was a slight shrug of his shoulders. "Your valet said you have been like this for a week. What has happened?"

At that, Rhys turned his head and looked Andrew in the eye. Could he truly be so oblivious? He stared Andrew down, trying not to be angry, trying not to care.

Andrew appeared to search his face for answers but came up with no solutions. Turning away he paced the room. Realization struck him as he saw the mementoes of Beatrice around the room. "Dear God! This is about Bea is it not? I never took you for a martyr!"

Rhys eyed Andrew in speechless astonishment. He should not

expect Andrew to understand. Beatrice had been rather nasty to Elinor. He would not take kindly to that either, were it his sister.

Andrew was still pacing. "Well, what is to be done? If you still want her, go and get her. The way Uncle described it he thought you were happy to have her off your hands. I am sure he would not stop you," he scoffed. "Relieved would be more like it."

"She does not want me," Rhys said with a raspy voice. He hesitated, having trouble forcing the words out. "It was her choice to leave."

"Beg pardon?" Andrew's pacing halted, and he turned abruptly to face Rhys. "She said that?" His face was struck with disbelief. "Have your wits gone begging?"

"Unfortunately, that is not the case." Rhys looked away, not wanting to see pity in his friend's eyes, and nodded. *She may not have said those words,* but her silence had implied as much to him when coupled with her indifference this Season. Andrew remained silent. There was little else to say after that. After a few long minutes, Rhys heard the door to the study click behind him. Andrew had decided to let him wallow in his misery after all. There was one benefit to knowing someone so well that they knew when to leave you to your wretchedness.

Rhys stared out of the window in despair after Andrew left. Winter. He loathed winter. The sky was dark and dreary; the wind was bitterly cold, and he hated being cold. The season fit his mood for once, however. He wondered what Beatrice was doing. Had she arrived yet? How was she getting on with his Aunt Mary?

Madness! You are torturing yourself. He tried in vain to remind himself that she was indifferent—that she did not return his affection. He grasped the letters and hesitated before throwing them in the fire. He watched eleven years of his life go up in flames. He picked up the whisky decanter and threw it against the wall. There was something to be said for venting your frustrations.

Beatrice sat in the swaying, crowded coach shivering, wretched, and smothering sobs. She knew them to be useless, but she could not control the tears. How could she do this? How could she not? She refused to return home and grovel. She could throw herself from the coach...

"What's wrong with ye? Ye ain't gonna wail like that the whole way to Lunnon, are ye?" Beatrice's sobs halted when she realized the voice was directed at her. A hiccough escaped her. "Oh Lord, are you increasing? Ye got yerself ruint and yer going to be sick the whole way!"

Beatrice peeked over her handkerchief at the prim older matron and her husband who were looking down their noses at her, lips pursed. "Shove her head out the door if she starts to look green, Percy." The matron elbowed her son to her left, who was occupied feeding his overstuffed face with a foul-smelling concoction that reeked of onions.

Vulgar mushroom! Beatrice bit back an acid reply. How dare they look down at her! The old biddy made a point of turning away from her and pointing her nose in the air as if she were a duchess. Beatrice laughed to herself at the irony. From the ballroom to banished in mere hours. She was obliged to acknowledge why they might assume the worst; she had no maid to lend her respectability, and her clothes were that of a female in reduced circumstances.

Beatrice ventured a glance at the other occupants of the coach, though it was difficult wedged into the seats. There was a young mother stealing a nap while her sleeping babe was resting on her shoulder. To the other side, a young man, well dressed, was propped against the squabs and snoring, his long legs and arms consuming most of her allotted space. She was feeling green, but from the atrocious odours and from feeling hemmed in, not from being with child.

She sighed. There was nothing to occupy her save her wretched thoughts. It was to be a long trip to Scotland, especially in the dead of winter, and she could not cry the entire journey. The man next to her shifted position and deposited his head on her shoulder with a thud. She jumped at the contact and tried to swallow a shriek, but perceived there was nothing to be done. She shook with trepidation. This was to be her life—for a time at least. She was at her father's mercy, and if she were well behaved, perhaps this foray into penury would be brief.

Beatrice tried to turn her attention to the scenery, which was thankfully indicating their imminent arrival in London. She had to hope that the passengers in the mail-coach would be smaller and more agreeable. Her mind wandered back to the last time she was in London and debated what would happen if she did not board the Mail. Could she find Rhys and beg forgiveness? Why had she not stopped him from leaving? There was a simple answer: pride.

Beatrice was too proud to admit her feelings for him and her life-long jealousy of her cousin had triggered unconscionable actions. She shook her head. No. She would prove that she could be as good as Elinor. Her whole life her father had compared her to Elinor, and wanted her to be like her. They would have to learn to accept her as she was. She had lost her taste for trying to be what others wanted.

She had just traded one hell for another. The mail coach was faster and took fewer passengers, but she had to sit forward, which disturbed her on the winding, steep roads. After hearing about the near misses on the narrow cliffs, she was somewhat thankful for not being able to see ahead. Queasy, frightened and crowded, she had to take deep breaths through her mouth to stop the nausea and panic. A large older man who spoke no English, and who did not bathe regularly, consumed most of her allotted space. Sharing her journey was a governess with two unruly children who threw tantrums, fought or screamed alternately. The only reprieve was a nice girl across from her who remained blissfully quiet. She had never abided confined space well, and this was no exception. The walls seemed to be closing in on her. She tried to think of happy thoughts and look out of the window, but there was so little to think on in that regard. Was she going to have to start a new life? Would she ever be welcomed back? What would Rhys do? She would never forget the look of disappointment on his face when he walked away from her.

The carriage slowed, jerked a few times, tipped up on its side, then stopped with a lurch. Everyone looked around as if to ascertain the problem when the guard and passengers jumped off to push, to no avail. Apparently they were stuck. The guard commanded everyone to exit. Slowly they each made their way out of the coach into the knee-deep snow. The coach was embedded in a snowdrift. As Beatrice stood to the side and watched the men attempt to dislodge the carriage, there were no words for the cold that spread over her body. She looked around at those who had been riding outside and suddenly felt extremely grateful for her cramped inside space.

She noticed the governess struggling to hold her two charges out of the snow and surprised herself by asking if she could be of assistance. The governess willingly availed herself of one of the boys, who would have preferred to jump into the snow and play. He squirmed and tried to wriggle his way out of her arms. Unsure of what to do, Beatrice wrapped her arms around him tight and threatened him as her nurse had used to do. "If you do not stop fighting, I will rap your knuckles!"

The boy looked at her wide-eyed and determined but realized she was serious, for he stopped fighting. He turned his energies toward other things, however, such as wiping his runny nose on her pelisse and trying to pull the ribbons from her bonnet. There was one redeeming part of helping with the boy—it saved her from having to help push the coach.

Eventually, the coach was freed from the rut, but now all of the passengers were wet and shivering. She was unable to imagine what the others must feel, or not feel, riding for hours without reprieve from the bone-chilling wind and cold. Hopefully, they were more prepared than she for the weather. When they climbed back into the carriage, she welcomed the body heat from the large, odorous foreigner. It had only been four-and-twenty hours since she had left home, and she no longer knew who she was or what she should do. All of her life, almost all decisions had been made for her. She was scared and frightened of what was to become of her. Nothing had prepared her for this swift taste of reality. As the cold continued to pervade her body, she found she was too tired and cold to care any longer and finally managed to drift off into a self-preserving sleep.

~

Beatrice was beginning to despair of ever reaching Scotland. Was there such a thing as coach fever? She wavered between shock and anger at her new circumstances most of the way. Over ninety hours of travelling in the tiny coach with barely a foot of space to call her own. The heavy fog and snowfalls had slowed the normal speed of the mail-coaches. Her nerves were frazzled, she was deprived of any meaningful sleep and she was hungry for a proper meal—not the abominable food vendors sold at the opportune changes of horses along the route. She had counted thousands of sheep along the way and hoped to never see another one of the woolly creatures again. If her father had hoped to prove a point, well, she felt lots of points aching all over her. And she smelled foul. She could not remember a time when she had ever felt so unclean, battered and forlorn. She attempted to suppress her melancholia by daydreaming of the long hot bath awaiting her when she arrived.

When the carriage pulled to a stop at long last, she found she had difficulty moving her stiff, numb and frozen legs. If she never had to view the inside of a passenger coach as long as she lived, it would be too soon. The snow was deep, and she gathered her frozen bag and made her way into the coaching inn. She desperately hoped there would be someone waiting for her to take her to her new... home? Post? She was unsure what this place would be to her. She found a warm spot by the fire and watched, waiting and hoping for news of someone who would be there to retrieve her. She lost heart when the last of the passengers left and the parlour was virtually empty.

She tried her best not to be disappointed. The past few days had proffered more life experience than her prior nineteen years combined. She sighed and bent to her bag to search for the letter with the directions to her final destination. She finally found what she was searching for: *Alberfoyle Priory*. She approached the inn keeper and asked for his assistance. "Sir?"

An older man with a head of grey hair and a bushy beard turned around from his task and looked at her. "Would you be so kind as to tell me how to find passage to Alberfoyle Priory? It seems no one came to meet me."

The old man snorted. "Aye. Ye might be able to find someone ye ken hire to take ye. But snows be verra deep 'an it be another long ride up the mountain in the snow."

Beatrice tried not to cringe. "Would you be so kind as to direct me?"

"Aye." She stood there and waited, wondering if the man would speak any more. He put a few things away behind the bar, then slowly walked toward a back door. He turned to see if she was following, and she hurried after him into the ankle-deep snow. He crossed to the stable yard and entered. He began speaking in hushed debate with the other men, with periodic glances at her. Beatrice stayed back, not wanting to intrude, acutely aware of her sordid appearance. Eventually, the innkeeper looked toward her and said that one of the men would drive her for two pounds.

"Two pounds?" Beatrice still did not understand much about economizing, but that was more than she had paid for the entire coach journey from the south coast of England!

"Ye can wait until someone comes through headed that way, but I canna say when that might be. With the heavy snows this winter, this might be yer best chance for days." He shrugged and turned to walk away, apparently indifferent to her concerns.

"Very well." She walked toward the man indicated, and he led her toward a small pony cart. She gritted her teeth and kept reminding herself everything would be better when she finally made it to the priory. She climbed into the small, open two-seat conveyance and braced herself. Well, now she would get to experience riding with the elements.

CHAPTER 4

Over a sennight had passed since the ball that changed Rhys' life. Sitting at home licking his wounds was not improving his disposition. He had wallowed in pity long enough. He resolved to leave the house today and try to move on. He was declaring his mourning period officially over. He surveyed himself in the glass— still the same wavy hair and chocolate eyes. So why did he feel so different?

He rang for his valet and was met with an undisguised sigh of relief when he asked Samuels to ready him for an outing. After washing and shaving, he dressed in a manner more á la mode than he felt.

He decided to walk to his club instead of riding, needing to fully immerse himself in reality. He stepped onto the pavement and was met with a blast of bitter cold. He debated going back in but shook his head and forced himself onward. He paused when he turned onto St. James's Street, but managed to continue placing one foot in front of the other. Perhaps the club would be slow and he could ease himself back into Town life. Dare he hope none of his friends would be there to harangue him about his absence?

No such luck. The club was brimming with people. The door-keeper managed to keep the look of curiosity from his face, but no one else bothered to try as he made his way past, making sport of speculating on his absence. He heard Andrew's voice from behind, "You look considerably better than you did last time I saw you. I should thank you for saving me the trip to check on you."

Rhys turned around and managed a small smile. "Pleased to oblige, Abbott." He spotted his other friend Easton sitting near Andrew and nodded a greeting. "What, the honeymoon over already? You are the last person I expected to see here."

Easton flashed him a big smile. "We only came to Town for business. I am not so moonstruck that Elly cannot shop without my presence."

"Accept my compliments," Rhys quipped.

Andrew spoke up, "What returns you to the land of the living?"

"Yes, Andrew was debating tactics on removing you from your home as we sat here." Easton chuckled. "The current idea was to pull you up by your bootstraps."

"Well, here I am, and all your debating was for naught. Have you made plans to deal with Fairmont?" Rhys asked as he signalled the waiter to bring some tea.

Andrew and Easton exchanged glances then simultaneously shook their heads.

"You do not mean to let him go scot-free?"

"We gave Elly our word that we would not retaliate," Andrew said, clearly frustrated.

"And you can accept that? I made no such agreement!" Rhys exclaimed, stirring his tea furiously.

"I think it best we abide by her wishes for now. She is the one who has suffered, and she feels that retaliation will make it worse. He has been making himself scarce, so if he behaves I am determined to be civil," Easton said quietly.

Rhys looked doubtful but shrugged his shoulders. He would not guarantee anything, but he was still too mentally exhausted to contemplate Nathaniel for now.

"Will you be attending the dinner the Dowager Duchess is holding tomorrow?" Easton inquired.

"Still celebrating?" Rhys quizzed.

"She says we must celebrate with our London friends." Andrew scoffed.

"I suppose that is as good a time as any to put myself back on the marriage market," Rhys said resignedly.

Andrew choked on his drink. "You are roasting us!"

"I am in earnest. I intend for this time around to be strictly business. I need an heir, which requires a wife, and I intend to be logical in my choice." He sipped his tea and avoided eye contact.

This declaration was met with silence from both of his friends.

"Know of any eligible partís?" It being out of season, the choices would be last year's leftovers.

Still silence. Rhys continued, "Perhaps your aunt would not mind introducing me to her triplets?" Lady Ashbury was known to be most particular about her daughters. He turned directly toward Easton as he spoke. "They are handsome and are well-bred. My only other requirement is that they be able to hold a conversation. That should be easy enough to determine. I suppose if that is not possible, they could play music during dinner," he said thoughtfully.

"Yes, well, they will be in attendance tomorrow evening. You may begin your logical choosing then, if you like," Easton said clearly amused.

Rhys set his tea cup down. "Either of you inclined to join me for a round at Gentleman Jackson's? I am running to fat after a fortnight of idleness."

"And you wish to display to advantage to chase the petticoats?" Andrew asked in disbelief.

"Perhaps. And I am itching to pummel someone."

"No need to explain. I will join you." Andrew set his glass down and rose to join Rhys.

They looked enquiringly toward Easton, and he shook his head. "I have been pummelled enough in my day. You two enjoy yourselves. I am due to meet Elly and the Dowager soon, in any case."

"Are you sure you are ready to commit yourself to leg-shackles, Vernon?" Andrew punched him playfully. They said their goodbyes and headed toward Jackson's.

After a few hours of steep, snowy tracks, the cart pulled into the gates of the priory. Beatrice could hardly muster excitement for her teeth chattering, her frozen bones and her eyes watering from the bitter cold. They travelled on through a thickly forested drive. When they finally pulled up to the house, it did not look like she thought a convent would. The sun was setting behind a large three-storey grey stone manor house. The mansion was tucked into the side of a mountain overlooking Loch Ken. If she were not frozen from the elements, she would have found the scene enchanting. Her curiosity was momentarily aroused, but she was too anxious to warm up to ponder the point too long.

She forced her stiff body from the pony cart. At least the driver was kind enough to hand her bag down to her. She waded through the deep snow to the front door and lifted the knocker. There were no signs of life that she could detect from here, though she thought she had seen smoke from some chimneys as they pulled up the drive. Apparently there was no one to answer the door. What kind of convent was this? She turned to the driver, somewhat surprised that he had not left already. "You are certain this is the right place?"

"Aye, miss. Ye might try the back."

"The back?" The back is for servants! He turned his gaze downward as his reply. She supposed the back door would be better than standing out here freezing. She could not feel her fingers and toes as it was. She climbed back into the cart, and he drove to the back door. Here, there were indications of inhabitance at least. She knocked on the door, and a servant girl opened it and eyed her sceptically.

"Is this the convent?" Beatrice asked.

"This ain't no convent. Ye must have the wrong place." The girl made to close the door.

"This is not Alberfoyle Priory?" Beatrice almost had to shove her foot in the door.

"Aye." The girl stopped and looked at her questioningly. "Ye must be the girl the Master were sending for the orphanage. Follow me."

"Orphanage?" Beatrice questioned, but the servant must not have heard.

Beatrice dismissed the driver and paid him the exorbitant two pounds, before following the servant up the narrow back stairs. She was shown to a small, sparse room with no fire. Her dressing room at home could have fit several rooms of this size inside! The servant began to recite routines and point to where to find things, but Beatrice was unable to comprehend what the girl was saying. It might as well have been a foreign language for all she understood. She thought the girl said she was supposed to retrieve her own water and coals for the fire. She had spent what felt like a week on a small, crowded coach. She was positive she had frostbite, and all she wanted was a hot bath. And now, she was expected to do all of this herself? "You must be mistaken!" was all she could say before she slumped on to the floor and began to sob.

"Lawks! What did I say? Is something the matter with ye?" The girl knelt down beside her and timidly began to pat her on the back, which only made Beatrice sob harder.

"I-I, just wanted a hot bath," she inhaled loudly several times, trying to stop crying, "and I have no idea what you are saying or how to do any of it."

She looked up at the girl through her tears and saw a dumbstruck look on her face. "Ye do not ken how te do any of it?" Beatrice shook her head and started to cry again. "Then why are ye here?"

"Be-be- ca-ca—" She emitted a loud hiccough then managed to say, "Because my father is angry with me."

"Did ye get into mischief?" The girl narrowed her eyes and put her hands on her hips. "Because Miss Mary willna tolerate any of that. Ye'd be better off leaving before she finds out."

"N-not that kind." Beatrice buried her head in her knees. "An unfortunate misunderstanding."

"Well, I'll help ye tonight, but ye will have te do fer yerself after that. Ye best tell me what happened, or I willna be able te help ye." She stood to help Beatrice up. "Come on then, me name is Addie."

"I am Beatrice," she replied, still trying to regain her composure.

Addie took Beatrice's hand to lead her back down the stairs. Addie stopped suddenly, turned and grabbed Beatrice's other hand and felt both of them. Feeling her soft, unworked hands, she looked up. "Ye truly have not done this before have ye? Who are ye?"

"I would rather not say." That came out sharper than she intended. Beatrice had never felt ashamed of who she was before, but she did not want to be judged by this servant, for she knew she would be found lacking.

Addie let out a whistle and shrugged her shoulders. "Verra well, if that's how ye want it."

They continued down the narrow stairs in silence until they reached the kitchen.

"Addie, do you mind telling me where I am? I thought I was being sent to a convent."

"Now, I see why ye might think that with the name priory, but this is just a hunting box for the Master, though he only fishes here. The name comes from the old priory down next to the loch. He is opening an orphanage here and the children are due to start arriving soon. Maybe he wants ye te be the governess or somethin'? Why else would a gently bred miss be sent here?"

"So, I am to help with children?" That was better than being a servant Beatrice thought to herself. But, she had no idea what to do with children. Maybe it would not be so difficult.

Once back down in the kitchen, Addie stoked the fire and grabbed two buckets off the wall. She proceeded to grab a cape and turned to Beatrice and indicated for her to do the same.

"We have to go back out there?" Beatrice looked at Addie and tried not to burst into tears again. Her face, hands and feet were still burning trying to warm up from being out there earlier.

"Where do ye think the water comes from? Ye have te refill what yer going te use." Addie shook her head.

Well, that made sense. Beatrice had never thought about where the water came from before. Someone always brought her some if she needed it.

"The well is frozen over right now. So we just have te scoop up some snow." Addie pointed far away to the well. "When 'tisn't frozen ye will get yer water over there."

That's nice, Beatrice thought. She did not plan on being here when the spring thaw happened, however. Addie scooped her bucket through the snow and motioned for Beatrice to do the same. That looks simple, she thought. But when she tried to pick it back up it was extremely heavy. She glanced over at Addie and saw her lips quivering. She turned back toward the bucket, more determined than ever, and with a big heave, lifted the bucket and promptly fell backward into the snow.

Addie could hold back her laughter no longer. She laughed and laughed but did come over and lend Beatrice a hand up out of the snow. Beatrice managed to pick her bucket up and walk with it awkwardly into the kitchen, not finding the situation amusing at all.

Addie set the buckets aside near the fire, took a towel and pulled the hot water from the fire, and replaced it with one of the buckets of snow. She pulled a hip-bath out of the cupboard and then poured the warm water into it. She set a screen around the bath and then turned to Beatrice.

"Here ye go. Ye'll need te clean up when yer finished. Then get yerself te bed. Morning comes early around here, and yer tasks are going te take longer since ye do not ken what yer doing."

"I am to bathe in the kitchen?" Beatrice shrieked.

"When yer lucky enough to get a bath." Addie turned to walk off.

Drat! She needed to remember where she was and not alienate this girl who was helping her.

"Addie, thank you for helping me." She had never thanked a servant before, but she desperately needed a friendly face here.

Addie sighed and turned back to look at her. "Some advice?" Beatrice nodded. "Do not complain about anything." She turned back and walked to the stairs.

Beatrice watched after her. What would she have to complain about? Once morning arrived, and they sorted out who she was, she would not have to worry about these things. She shrugged and managed to get herself out of her clothing and into the water, choosing not to dwell on anything other than the bath for now.

CHAPTER 5

The next morning, Beatrice felt a tap, tap, tap on her shoulder. She was too cold to ponder moving, let alone wake up.

"Beatrice! It's Addie. Ye better get out of bed quick!"

"Why have they not lit the fire? It is freezing in here." She spoke through her steaming breath and chattering teeth, pulling her coverlet closer.

"So ye do not ken how te make a fire either? 'Tis a wonder ye did not freeze te death during the night. Ye forgot te clean up yer mess in the kitchen as well."

Beatrice crawled out of bed, disorientated and aching all over. Addie was searching for her clothes, then noticed the portmanteau still unpacked on the floor.

"Lawks! Ye dinna unpack yer bag neither!" Addie shook her head in bewilderment. "Ye is going te have a rough time here, Beatrice. I'll get ye one of me dresses, but ye need te have yer clothes washed and ironed before ye goes te bed."

Why did she feel like a reprimanded four-year-old? Beatrice was certain her governess had never been required to do such things. Was she expected to know all of this? Addie left and returned quickly with a dress for Beatrice. It was several inches too short and snug on Beatrice's feminine form. "It will have te do fer now. We're about te miss breakfast. Ye will have te take care of yer laundry and empty yer chamber pot after breakfast," Addie said breathlessly as they hurried down the stairs. "Miss Mary will want te meet with ye and give ye yer duties."

Beatrice was struck speechless. Did the girl just say empty her chamber pot? Was Addie jesting? Or was she caught in an awful dream she could not wake from? "There must be some mistake here."

"Mebbe. But I'm grateful for a position with a warm place te sleep an' food te eat."

Beatrice was not warm, and she had not eaten.

They hurried into the kitchen and to the table. Addie silently pointed to a seat for her as everyone at the table stared openly at Beatrice. Did they expect her to eat with the servants?

Apparently. The woman at the end of the table looked her up and down. "Yer late."

Beatrice stared back at the woman. What did she expect her to say? The woman hesitated, then told everyone to sit. Everyone obeyed in silence, including Beatrice, but the looks of curiosity did not stop. Beatrice was unsure of the protocol at the servants' table, so she tried to mimic what Addie did. The food was simple, and she was not sure what all of it was, but she found she was too hungry to care.

When all of the servants had finished eating, Cook rose, and the other servants stood immediately. Beatrice was so unused to the order of the downstairs staff she did not realize she was supposed to stand. Addie was desperately motioning for her to rise, but it was too late. The other servants began to stare and snicker until Cook dismissed them, except her, of course.

"Yes?"

"Yer hair is a mess, yer dress doona fit, yer late, ye left a mess in me kitchen and ye doona have manners."

Her hair. Beatrice felt her ratted hair subconsciously. She had never done her own hair, but she would have attempted it had she remembered. Her hair was difficult to tame with a full-time maid. She could only imagine how it appeared now. She had no desire to make excuses to the Cook so she remained silent. She would find Miss Mary and straighten this misunderstanding out—after she combed her hair.

"Ye have nothing te say, eh? Then go te yer tasks before I give ye more."

Beatrice turned to walk up the stairs as Cook muttered under her breath about idle, lazy, spoiled misses.

After Beatrice walked out, Mary, Lord Vernon's aunt, stepped into the room from where she had been observing in the hallway. "I cannot fathom what my nephew saw in her. It seems she has come by her just desserts! Let us hope she makes a better lady than servant."

"I dinna ken ye meant for her te be a servant. That will be a disaster 'an more work fer everybody. She is a waste of our time. Her da will just come pick her up in a few weeks anyhow."

"It was not my intention to have her be a servant, but since events have unfolded in that manner, I think it perhaps worthwhile to allow her to work her way up. Perhaps by doing the work of servants she will appreciate the ones around her more in the future. I do not wish to thrust more work on you. However, if you can tolerate a few more days I would like to humble her just a bit more."

"Aye. If I ken it's just a few more days I can make shift. I can fancy depressing her pretensions. Just doona expect me te feel sorry fer the lass."

"I will admit she is a hard one to like, but we must not judge. I must keep reminding myself who her mother was. It is our God-given duty to teach her what she has neglected to learn," Mary said, despite her obvious displeasure in the task. "I cannot believe my nephew would be so blind."

"It happens te the best of 'em," Cook said sympathetically.

Beatrice's mind was spinning in a thousand directions as she attempted to plait her own tangled hair. She was still reeling from having to empty her chamber pot when a maid summoned her to meet with Miss Mary. The girl saw her struggling with her hair and quickly came over and finished the plait and tucked it up into a knot.

Beatrice followed the girl to a parlour, then entered and looked around. This was the first she had seen of the main part of the house. Not ostentatious or of the latest mode, but certainly not shabby. The room was lighter and more feminine than the rest of the house, with comfortable sofas and a vase of fresh flowers. She was somehow reminded of her grandmother, the Dowager Duchess, in this space.

An older woman, dressed in drab grey with her hair pulled into a severe chignon, looked her over critically. She was clearly assessing what she had been told of Beatrice with what she saw before her. This must be Miss Mary. Beatrice's hopes sank.

The woman cleared her throat and began, "Pray, do not imagine who you are will be of any consequence here. You will simply be Beatrice. You will have to do your part while you are here. We are short of staff until the house parents arrive, and with the orphanage opening soon, I daresay you will be needed there when your duties here are finished." She cleared her throat again, and then walked around the room with her hands behind her back, not bothering to see how her words were received. Beatrice had not forgotten her manners, however, and offered a curtsy when the woman bothered to face her.

After a cold stare, the woman continued, "Your father intends for you to learn appreciation and humility, among other things. Knowing your mother, I understand where your lack of education in this quarter came from. Still, there will be no excuses. It will not be tolerated here. We all earn our keep. I run the household with the assistance of a few maids and Cook. There are some men who work in the stables and on the land. I trust you will behave in that regard. You may earn back privileges with good behaviour. I will be reporting back to the Duke on a weekly basis."

"What is your plan for me?" Beatrice barely managed to speak, stunned. She had hoped her place in the house had just been a mistake. But as she watched this horrid woman, she began to feel sorely used. A convent would be preferable to this Turkish treatment!

"The Master thought you could be of use with the orphanage,

perhaps as a governess. I do not feel gossip and fashion are useful subjects for these children, however. We will see what you can learn in the next few weeks, and I will place you accordingly."

This is temporary. Keep telling yourself. Do not complain. Beatrice smiled through gritted teeth, trying to restrain the resentment seething within. "And who is this Master everyone speaks of? You act as if he knows me."

"You are impertinent, young lady. In my day, we did not speak in such a manner to our elders."

In her day? Indeed. The woman looked like she was on borrowed time, and she was cold enough to freeze hell over. Beatrice offered a smile that was as sickly sweet as she felt inside.

"You will find out in due time about the Master. He visits every summer after the Season. He is an old family friend of your father's. He is taking you in as a favour." She dismissed the topic with a wave of her hand. "Addie will help teach you the basics, and you will start in the kitchen with Cook."

Her favourite person. A nervous titter escaped.

"Please save your false antics for London's drawing rooms. They are decidedly unwelcome here. You are dismissed for now," Miss Mary said sharply.

Like a common servant.

"Ye are te be with me in the kitchen fer now," the cook said as she handed Beatrice an apron. "Miss Mary is not sure where te put ye yet. I doubt you will last here, but I'll give ye a chance. Take a basket from over there," she pointed to a shelf, "then gather the eggs and fetch me a chicken."

Gather eggs? That sounded manageable. She grabbed the basket off the shelf and donned the cape and boots she had worn to fetch the snow the night before. But where did one gather eggs? She was sure they were outside, but where?

"Pardon me, Cook?"

"What now?" She looked up with a scowl, then back to the dough she was kneading.

"Where do I gather the eggs?"

Cook looked up impatiently to see if Beatrice was teasing her. Seeing the look on Beatrice's face was answer enough.

Cook muttered under her breath. "The hen house perhaps?"

"And where might this hen house be?" Beatrice asked too politely. She would not be deterred. If they wanted her to be a servant, then they would have to teach her how.

Cook muttered again and turned away. "Just a few days. Just a few days." She turned back around. "Next te the barn. Ye do ken what a barn is?"

Beatrice pushed through the door before she snapped back at Cook. She had to behave so she could leave this God-forsaken place with its God-forsaken inhabitants. She pulled her cape tight and stomped toward the barn near the stables. She spied a smaller building near the barn and headed toward it. She opened the door and was accosted by a stench and chickens. She immediately closed the door and threw herself in front of it. She had to go in there with live chickens to gather the eggs? This surpassed all. She was terrified of animals. They always bit her or defecated on her. She took several deep breaths. It would be too humiliating to go back without the eggs, when they were all waiting for her to fail. She turned and opened the door again and pinched her nose this time. She looked around, and there were dozens of chickens walking around clucking and pecking. Disgusting. There were faeces everywhere on the floor mixed with hay, and chickens were pecking at her feet. "Ohh!" she shrieked and jumped into the air, and tried to shoo the chickens away with the basket, never abandoning the hold on her nose.

Now where the devil were the eggs? Beatrice looked around and saw more chickens up on the wall in boxes, but she could not see any eggs. She was afraid to walk further into the hen house, but she was more afraid to return without eggs. Maybe someone in the stables could tell her where the eggs were.

Outside, she was grateful to leave the chickens and breathe

through her nose again. Beatrice shut the door and began walking toward the stables. As she neared the stalls, she heard voices.

"Did ye see 'er hair?" a female voice said laughingly, "That's the problem with these fine ladies. Never had te do nothin' for themselves."

"'ow do you ken she's a fine lady?" a male voice asked.

"I can spot 'em a mile away! 'Er hands and skin are perfect, an' it's the way she acts. I'd stake my month's wages she ain't never lifted a finger before."

"I bet she got herself ruint and was sent 'ere te hide it." A different female voice offered her opinion.

"Well, she can ruin herself with me any time!" All the males laughed.

Beatrice had heard enough. She should not be surprised they were gossiping about her, but it stung nonetheless. "I hate to interrupt this *tête-à-tête*, but would someone mind showing me where the eggs are?" She flashed her most charming smile, refusing to let them see her bothered. She had been brought up by a duchess after all.

One of the grooms answered quickly, "I'll show you that an' more, sweetheart!"

Beatrice screamed and jumped. One of the chickens had stowed away in her basket and had decided to perch on her arm.

"Get it off! Get it off!" she screamed.

"Stay calm, miss, I'll fetch it fer ya." She stood still, fighting to control her shaking. Another groom placed the chicken back in the basket and led her back toward the hen house. As they walked away, the remaining servants continued laughing.

"Ignore 'em. Just work hard, and they will leave ye be." He shoved his hands in his pockets. "I am Tommy, and if someone bothers ye, just come find me."

"Thank you, Tommy. I am Beatrice." She looked down. "I cannot blame them for laughing. I *have not* ever lifted a finger before."

"There is no time like now." Tommy opened the door to the hens. Beatrice immediately pinched her nose, and Tommy had to stifle a laugh. He picked the rogue hen up out of the basket and walked over

45

to the nesting boxes on the wall. He felt around inside them and began to pull eggs out.

"That's where the eggs are, miss. Just go through each one and get the eggs out. That's it. Now I best be getting back te my own work."

"Thank you again, Tommy." She flashed him a warm smile.

He tipped his hat, a blush forming on his cheeks. "My pleasure."

Beatrice turned back toward the nesting boxes. Still pinching her nose, she set the basket down and put her hand into a nesting box. Two eggs! She could do this, she thought excitedly. Though thoroughly disgusted by the filth covering the eggs, she managed to go through each of the boxes and put the eggs in her basket. She came to the last one, and there was a hen still sitting in the box.

She muttered to herself, "Am I supposed to reach under the hen?" She reached gingerly around the hen, hoping she would not notice her.

No such luck. The hen began pecking Beatrice's arm. She shrieked and stepped backwards and fell onto the basket full of eggs. She heard the crunch and immediately began to cry.

She pulled herself up covered in yellow slime, picked up the basket and got out of there as quickly as possible.

Halfway back to the house, she finally stopped crying, and she glanced over at the basket only to find the same hen sitting in there again on top of the broken eggs. She kept on to the house. She would leave whatever eggs she could salvage, then take the chicken back.

She walked into the kitchen, and when Cook saw her, she looked like she would have an apoplexy.

"What in the…?" She looked at the basket in wonderment, "Ye got the eggs and a chicken too? I'll be…"

She scarcely heeded what Beatrice looked like, she was merely surprised Beatrice had done what she was told. Beatrice had completely forgotten about bringing a chicken. Thank heaven for small favours.

"I might have broken a few of the eggs," Beatrice said solemnly.

"Frankly, I dinna reckon ye te get any, so one is better than I expected." Cook dusted off her hands and walked around the table to come see the basket of eggs. "Help me clean 'em, then you can go wring and pluck the chicken."

"Pardon?" Beatrice said.

Cook shook her head. "Never mind. I'll show ye after we wash the eggs."

When the eggs were clean, Beatrice had never been so tired in her life. She knew this was just the beginning of the day, and she already needed a bath and a nap.

There were not many eggs that survived the mishap, but Beatrice was still proud of herself anyway.

"Fetch the chicken, and we'll prepare it for roasting," Cook directed.

Beatrice looked down at the chicken that had not left her side since she entered the hen house this morning, and suddenly felt dismal. She was sure she knew what was coming. She had never thought about how the chicken made it to her plate, and she began to feel queasy. The little pecker had grown attached to Beatrice, and she did not want to see it be served for dinner.

"Cook, do you think this chicken too small?" Beatrice asked shyly.

Cook spun around and gave Beatrice a look with her hands on her hips. "Now missy, doona be telling me ye've gone and attached yerself to that bird, have ye? Just like a spoilt miss to be having affection for her dinner."

Beatrice looked sheepish. "I know it does not signify, but I have never had an animal take a fancy to me before."

Cook, threw up her hands. "Fine, but ye have te go fetch another one. And ye canna keep that one in here."

Beatrice smiled and shooed the hen back into the basket. She skipped a step as she went back out of the door feeling like she had won a small victory. *I am reduced to being delighted about a chicken*, she thought. She made it back to the hen house, still detesting the smell. She set her new friend down and began to search for another chicken. Apparently the little hen was an anomaly, because when Beatrice got close to any of the others, they would flap their wings and squawk and claw violently at her.

This became a game of chase the chicken. Beatrice finally resorted to tackling one of the chickens and wrapping it in her skirt. She had lost all dignity. She ran back to the kitchen and dropped the chicken on the floor as fast as she could.

Cook looked up and burst into laughter. She laughed hysterically until she was crying. Beatrice just stood there and watched. She was covered in feathers, hay and God knows what else. And all Cook could do was laugh at her. She had not even been there a whole day, and she was a complete failure.

Cook finally stopped laughing, reached down and took the chicken by the leg, held it upside down, and the blasted thing looked like it went to sleep. Beatrice was astonished. Cook grabbed a huge knife and told Beatrice to follow her. Beatrice could not even begin to ponder what the knife was for. Cook shook the bird upside down a few times and proceeded to hang the chicken by its feet on the clothes line. She grabbed the chicken's head and cut it off. Beatrice immediately retched.

Cook just shook her head. "Go and wash yerself. This will take a few minutes te drain then ye need te pluck it."

Dear God, she had entered hell. She ran up the stairs, shut the door to her room and fell on the floor sobbing. She knew herself to be lily-livered, but she had never had to experience anything like that before. She knew she had to return, but she longed to run away. She removed her sullied dress and pulled out a wrinkled one from her bag. *This will have to do for now*, she thought.

She had no water in her basin. She supposed that was something else she had to do for herself. She made her way back down to the kitchen, still feeling green. "May I have some water to wash?"

Cook took a little pity on her and nodded her head toward the water basin. "I'll put the chicken in the boiling water for ye so it will be ready te pluck when yer finished."

Beatrice was tempted to empty her stomach again, but she took a deep breath and nodded her head. She felt a little better with cold water splashed on her face. She went back over to Cook reluctantly.

Cook pulled the headless chicken out of the boiling water and began to show her how to pluck the feathers.

She tried not to think about what she was doing and, with Cook helping, the task was over with quickly. Cook placed the chicken on the spit and turned back to Beatrice. She pointed toward a bucket on the wall. *There's more?* Beatrice could not imagine.

"The cows need milking." Beatrice did not even ask any questions. With her head held low, she took the bucket from the wall and headed back to the barn.

CHAPTER 6

*R*hys checked his cravat in the looking glass. He still was not feeling quite the thing, but he felt he could pass muster. Samuels assisted him into his perfectly fitted coat and inspected it for lint. Satisfied, Rhys flipped a rogue wave of hair back from his forehead before heading downstairs. He was determined to be pleasant and begin the business of finding a wife that evening. He had forgotten to ask Andrew for hints about how to tell the triplets apart. He did not wish to embarrass himself when courting someone.

He climbed into his carriage, wishing this was over with. He hoped he could pick a girl tonight, take her for a ride in the park tomorrow and then ask her father for her hand the next day. Was that not how marriages of convenience worked? He thought he was generally considered quite a catch.

His carriage pulled up in front of the Duke's town-house. Rhys groaned. He had not even considered he would have to dine at Loring Place. He had assumed dinner to be at Easton's or the Abbotts'. He leapt from the carriage and pasted a false smile on his face, saying hello to the familiar Barnes as he entered the house.

The family was gathered in the parlour. He greeted everyone outwardly as his usual jovial self, but inside he kept expecting Beatrice to walk through the door at any moment. It felt as if he had spent as much time at this house as his own over the years.

He made meaningless prattle with the Dowager Duchess, who probably knew exactly what was on his mind but was polite enough to refrain from mentioning it. The Duchess, however, could barely look at him. He knew it would be heartless to flirt with other females in front of her, but he had no choice. He had already set aside eleven years for Beatrice, and he did not have more time to waste.

"Lord and Lady Ashbury and the Ladies Anjou, Beaujolais and Margaux." Barnes flawlessly announced the arrival of the party for which Rhys had been waiting.

Easton stood next to Rhys and spoke quietly, "Which eligible lady shall be the first object of your gallantry?"

Rhys replied blandly, "Surprise me."

Lady Ashbury walked over after greeting the hosts. "May I join in the conversation? Perhaps I might be of assistance."

"Beg pardon?" Rhys's eyebrows shot up. Surely Easton had not told his aunt?

"My nephew mentioned you would be interested in getting to know my daughters."

He had. Rhys looked at Easton, who was grinning with unabashed amusement at Rhys's discomfort. "You said you meant business. In my experience, it is best to go straight to the source."

Rhys could not argue with that. "I am much obliged to you." He bowed and kissed the hand that Lady Ashbury offered.

"Handsomely put." She smiled with laughter dancing in her eyes. "Shall we sit?" Rhys offered Lady Ashbury his arm and he led her to a settee.

"I confess, I cannot tell the triplets apart. I am afraid this will make becoming acquainted difficult."

"*Non-sens*. The more you become acquainted, the easier it will be. I will make it simple for you." She discreetly pointed to one of the girls. "Anjou is the eldest. She is the one wearing blue gauze. She has a tiny beauty spot near her left eye and her eyes are blue."

Rhys tried to take mental notes. He prayed he would not be quizzed about fabrics.

"Beaujolais is the one wearing rose satin, and her eyes are bluish-violet."

She waved her hand toward the third girl, who was wearing a green frock.

"I do not suppose Margaux has green eyes?"

Lady Ashbury laughed, then said, "Bluish-green."

"Do they always wear the same colours?" *That might make it easier,* he thought.

"*Non!* That would be a disaster!" She tapped him on the arm with her fan in mock reprimand.

He thought it a famous idea himself. Lady Ashbury was still speaking while he was trying to file away the differences between the threesome.

"As you know, we have kept the girls…how do you say, sheltered?"

Rhys nodded. He had heard that repeatedly from Andrew and in the clubs.

"I will say that none of the girls are betrothed. However, you might find your efforts best spent with Margaux."

Rhys looked up at the three beauties blankly. He still could not tell any difference between them, save the colour of their dresses. He thought Margaux was the green one.

Lady Ashbury continued, "Anjou is still heartsick from her soldier being sent to the American War, and Beaujolais has lately shown favouritism toward someone."

"Therefore, the logical choice is Margaux," Rhys finished for her.

"*Oui.*" She clapped her hands together. "You do see! This may be easier than I thought."

"So you are not opposed to my court of your daughter?"

"*Non.* She can hold her own. If she is not pleased with you, she will tell you."

Rhys smiled. Maybe this would not be unpleasantly flat after all.

"I have seen that you will be seated with her. Logical, *non?*"

"Indeed." Rhys thought for a moment. "Madame, does Lady Margaux know I am..."

"Dangling after her? *Non*." She shook her head. "That would be most illogical. Though, she is wise and will perceive your intentions quickly." Lady Ashbury rose, and Rhys stood beside her.

"You put me to the blush, madame." He bowed to her. "But I am much obliged, nevertheless."

"Let us hope for *beauté* from something *désagréable*," Lady Ashbury said quietly before walking away.

At dinner, everyone continued to act as if nothing was amiss, as if everything was normal, and Beatrice was not living in obscurity. One of the triplets was sitting in Beatrice's usual chair, the one with the blue dress and blue eyes, and he found he did not even want to look at her. At least, Margaux, the one in green, was seated next to him.

Rhys took a sip of his soup and tasted nothing. He was as nervous as a green boy. He had no idea what to say and blurted out the first thing that came to mind, "How does it feel to be a triplet?" He turned toward Margaux and she looked perplexed. "I beg your pardon. You will probably get asked that several times in an evening." He looked down and shook his head. He had taken for granted how well he had known Beatrice. Making débutante talk was completely foreign to him. He should probably just return home. His friends would roast him for days if they knew how ineloquent his speech was.

"Not at all. I have not been out much, so I have not been asked that many times. I am not sure how to answer you. I have never known anything but being a triplet."

"So it is the same as asking me how I like to be a single."

"Precisely." She laughed and he relaxed.

"It is fascinating to us singles, in case you were wondering. For example, what it is like to have two mirror images of yourself? Do you interchange with each other, and can the governess or your parents tell...forgive me. I cannot seem to remember how to conduct a proper dinner conversation."

"Hmm. Well," she contemplated the questions, ignoring his awkward speech, "I do not consider them mirror images. To me there are many differences between us. We fooled many nursemaids, but never our parents." She smiled.

"The eyes?"

She looked surprised. "How did you know?"

"I have my sources." He looked toward Lady Ashbury, who winked at him. He had to look down at his plate to hide another blush.

"Ah, *Maman*." She took a sip of her wine. "So do you prefer bluish, bluish-violet or bluish green?"

"All forms of bluish," he said without hesitation. He preferred hazel, but kept that to himself.

"Very diplomatic of you, but I do not care for flummery!"

"Consider me admonished, Lady Margaux." He smiled his roguish smile, and turned to his right to spend his allotted time with his other dinner partner.

However, the Duchess addressed Easton loud enough for all the guests to hear, "Lord Easton, how is your latest orphanage progressing?"

"I was just trying to convince Andrew and Duke of the merits of opening more. However, Vernon has converted his Scottish property, and it is due to open any day, as is our boarding school."

"Indeed?" The Duchess looked pointedly at Rhys, hoping for news about her daughter, he presumed. The Duchess always had a reason for everything she said or did. "Beatrice is visiting in Scotland."

Rhys tried not to grimace. Just as things were beginning to look hopeful, the conversation would drift toward Beatrice.

"Will you be going to visit the property soon?" the Duchess inquired.

Clever, Duchess, clever.

The Dowager coughed loudly to cover her sarcastic murmur of, "Very subtle."

The Duke coughed a warning.

"I visit every summer," Rhys answered pleasantly, but the Duchess already knew the answer.

"Yes, the trip would be insufferable this time of year, would it not?" A rhetorical question aimed at the Duke and Rhys.

Do not blame me, I saved her from the convent, Rhys thought. "I suppose it might be less pleasant at this time of year. My family has always visited after the Season, and I continue to do so."

"I think it is wonderful you are starting an orphanage. Are there many in need there? I see so many on the streets here, it is heartbreaking," Lady Ashbury said, diverting the conversation to less dangerous territory.

"There are people in need everywhere. I believe many of the children are coming from Glasgow and Dumfries," Rhys answered her.

"How many children are there?" Margaux asked, interested.

"We are to begin with twenty children. We plan on modelling it after the one Easton started here, as a safe, happy environment where the children may acquire skills that will be useful for them to employ when they leave."

"That is wonderful!" Anjou exclaimed.

"I cannot take credit. Easton is the mastermind." Rhys waved away the praise.

"Nonsense. I merely planted the idea, and Vernon did the rest. We have plans for more if anyone feels obliged to donate the funds or property," Easton replied unashamedly. Lord Ashbury and Easton went on into further conversation on the topic, while Rhys began to dread his trip to Scotland.

"We are here to celebrate Lord and Lady Easton. Shall we?" The wise Dowager Duchess chimed in, deciding to steer the conversation in a less threatening direction away from Beatrice.

Beatrice gingerly touched the still tender place over her swollen shut eye. She winced. She was thankful she had no looking-glass, for she feared she would not even recognize herself. How was she to know cows got angry when they were not milked on time? She had never been around the large beasts before. They were quite temperamental, in her opinion. Obviously, she did not know the first thing about them.

Addie had already been there milking, and Beatrice had tried to mimic her motions. Milking was much harder than it looked. She could not get any milk to come out, and this angered the cow, who stomped her feet and snorted at Beatrice. When Addie finally showed her how, she must have been going too slowly, for the cow kicked over the bucket, then managed to plant an angry hoof in her eye.

Once Beatrice stopped screaming from the pain and recalled what had happened, she tried to sit up and fell back over into the hay. Addie called for one of the stable boys, who scooped her up and ran with her back to the house. Cook took one look at Beatrice and had him place her on a sofa. She then placed a slab of raw meat over her eye. *Raw meat.* She tried not to cringe.

Miss Mary was called in to see if a doctor was needed, and her usual cool façade was replaced with an expression of worry. *Either I look horrendous, or she is worried about what my father will think,* Beatrice thought spitefully. She doubted he would bother to care.

"What happened?" Miss Mary questioned everyone standing there. Most of the servants had gathered around to stare at her.

Addie spoke up, "The cow kicked 'er when she was trying te milk it."

"I see. Perhaps it might be best to ask for help when you have not done something before, Beatrice?"

That was the final straw. Her head was swollen and throbbing, she did not know if she would ever be able to see again, and Miss Mary chose now to chastise her? Not, *is she going to be all right?* Her shock was over. Anger bubbled up inside her. They want to toy with her and make sport of her lack of expertise in service? She might have been killed!

Beatrice propped herself up on one arm and tried to look at them with her one eye that would open, "Do you want to know what I did wrong? I was born into privilege." Several of the servants gasped. "I gossiped, though no more than any of you have said of me. I hurt someone I should not have. That is my crime. Believe me, I have been punished. I have learned my lesson. I would, however, like to leave this place alive. I have tried to mind my tongue and work without complaint. Kindly have your laughs at someone else's expense." Beatrice laid her head back down, feeling as if it would explode following this ungracious speech.

Miss Mary stared at her long and hard, expressionless. She finally told one of the maids to send for the doctor and then quietly left the room. The servants slowly filed out, except for Addie, who sat next to her and squeezed her hand. "You poor dear. I will send for a restorative."

She was thankful for the unexpected comfort from her, but she was also so angry she could scream if it would not hurt so much. Mayhap writing a letter would help...

"Addie, do you think you could also acquire some paper and ink? I would like to write a letter."

Some time later, the doctor arrived and was escorted in by Miss Mary. Beatrice opened her unaffected eye and was shocked by what she saw. She had never seen a doctor who was not old with grey hair. This doctor could not be eight-and-twenty yet, and looked like an Adonis. Beatrice was suddenly very self-conscious. She had not cared what she looked like since she'd left Sussex, and suddenly she felt like a new débutante under inspection.

She realized the young doctor was speaking to her. "Pardon?"

Adonis smiled. "I am Gavin Craig." The doctor held out his hand.

She looked to Miss Mary, unsure of what to say. The older woman nodded. "I am Beatrice." She held her hand out to him. He felt her hand and raised an eyebrow, but did not say anything.

"I heard you met the wrong end of a cow. Would you mind if I take a look?" He smiled reassuringly.

Feeling uncharacteristically shy, she looked down and shook her head, but this made her dizzy and caused her to grimace in pain.

"Easy now, lass." He gently helped her lie her head back down and began to feel around her head and face. She jumped when he reached the bones around her eye.

"I am going to hold up some fingers now, lass. I want you to try to open your eyes and tell me what you can see." He began to hold different numbers of fingers up and moved them several directions. "Now follow the finger with just your eye."

She could not manage to open her right eye. But she was able to tell him how many fingers he was holding with her left.

He asked, "Do you hurt anywhere else?"

Beatrice thought for a minute then said, "No." Being careful not to shake her head again.

"All right then." He turned toward Miss Mary and addressed both of them, "I doona think she will have permanent damage, but it is too soon to tell with certainty. She needs to stay in bed as much as possible for the next few days. Fortunately, ice is plentiful this time of year. She needs to keep her head down and put ice on the eye several times a day. I will try to come back and see her when I can."

He bowed farewell to his patient and began to walk towards the door with Miss Mary.

"Sir," Beatrice called after him. "Will I look like this forever?"

"No, lass, I doona think so." He shook his head. "You should have your beautiful face back soon."

Miss Mary and the doctor walked out. Beatrice tried not to blush. She could not believe she had asked that. She overheard the doctor speaking to Miss Mary in the hallway.

"Make sure she stays in bed to keep the swelling from worsening. I also think it best to keep her away from the animals from now on."

Thank God someone has some sense, Beatrice thought gratefully. The doctor and Miss Mary continued talking as they walked off. Beatrice would love to know what the woman had told him, and she was already looking forward to his next visit.

~

Beatrice could not stand lying still one moment longer. She sat up slowly and swung her legs over the side of the bed. She must have slept for hours—or days. Someone had taken care to add coal to the fire and leave a tray. Beatrice rose to her feet, and the room spun. She held on to the bed post to steady herself then slowly made her way to the small desk by the fire. She lit the taper and tried to focus her good eye enough to write a letter.

She sat and pondered whether to write the letter or not. Would it serve any purpose? Her first inclination was to write to Rhys, but after the way they'd parted she doubted it would be welcome. How could a lifelong relationship deteriorate so quickly? She could not bear that he thought so little of her, and that stung enough to make her stay away, for it was about more than the one incident with Elly. Things had not been well with them for months, and she did not think the relationship would ever be the same, especially since he had walked away so easily. The ache of unhappiness that had settled in her heart throbbed anew at the recollection.

Sadly, she reflected, she did not actually have any other *real* friends. All of the other society connections were superficial. Any letter she wrote would be circulated and gossiped about. That was how the *ton* operated, and was all the more reason she felt her punishment unfair. She leaned her aching head on her hand and sighed.

She knew her mother would expect to hear from her, but she did not want to admit failure or complain. *It is what Father expects.* She would write something simple so the Duchess would be satisfied.

Dearest Mother,

I arrived in Scotland and am settling into my new home. The priory is much like any other country house, though it is set in the mountains. It is much colder here, and there is an abundance of snow. I never realized how deep snow could become!

That was not a lie, Beatrice thought, as she struggled for what to say.

I am meeting many new interesting people, although I have seen little of local society so far.

That was an understatement if she had ever made one.

There is a young doctor here, but he seems to be knowledgeable and is most agreeable. I have learned much about animals since arriving,

Mostly what she already assumed—to stay away from them.

And an orphanage will be opening here soon, which I shall be helping with.

Lord help them all. That should give her mother the vapours. Beatrice giggled but stopped quickly with pain.

She could not think of anything else to add, so she curled up on the bed and went back to sleep instead.

Mary joined Cook that evening for tea. Cook was still dumbfounded. "I dinna think it would get so out of hand. Who would think something as simple as milkin' a cow could go so wrong?"

"I should have expected this to happen." Mary held fingers to her temple, exasperated.

"Are ye going te tell her da?" Cook asked sceptically.

"I am undecided. He told me to use my judgement in teaching her some lessons. Dr. Craig believes she will recover." She took a sip of her tea. "The real question is, what will she tell her mother? I assure you, if she thinks her daughter ill-used, she will make it her mission to make the rest of my life miserable."

"I dinna ye ken her family." Cook looked surprised.

"Unfortunately, Wilhelmina and I have known one another since our first Season. I was betrothed to her brother before he died. I did not like her then, and the limited interaction we have had recently does not find her much improved. She has been trying to bring up her daughter to be just like her."

"I think the girl has more pluck than we give 'er credit for. She has not complained. I keep expectin' 'er te throw fits 'an tantrums, but she keeps tryin'."

"Perhaps I need to end this charade. I should not hold the sins of the mother against the daughter. I do not think this is what he had in mind when he sent her here for reformation, but I cannot just begin treating her like royalty either. *We* do not live that way."

"Just a little longer," Cook said. "She is making progress. The children will start arriving soon, 'an ye can focus on her helping there. Now that everyone ken she's a lady, they willna treat her the same anyway."

"They will do as they are told. I am more concerned with what will happen when my nephew arrives."

"I am surprised she doona ken who the Master is," replied Cook.

"That certainly would not help the situation. He did not think her to be here very long. Whatever put the notion in his head to send her here in the first place? He thought it best not to tell he was the owner, but I will not lie if asked."

"Verra well. I'll do what ye think is best," Cook said doubtfully.

"I am sure I do not know what that is."

CHAPTER 7

*R*hys and Andrew arrived to escort Lady Margaux and one of her sisters on an outing to the park. Rhys had asked Andrew to join them since he was always sitting in one of their pockets. Rhys still was not sure which triplet Andrew had his eye on. He made a mental note to explore that later.

Today, Beaujolais would be joining them. Perhaps she was the one Andrew had interest in. He hoped it was not Margaux. He did not want to let this business interfere with one of his oldest friendships. Andrew was unusually mum about it all. Perhaps that was out of allegiance to the old friendship they shared with Beatrice.

Thankfully, the weather was co-operating. It had been cold and wet for most of the winter, but today was mild and sunny. Evidently the rest of Society felt the same way, for the park was extremely crowded. Rhys had not considered the consequences of the outing, but he felt Margaux was turning out to be a satisfactory choice, so who they saw today was of little consequence.

Rhys became aware that he was wool-gathering when the others began laughing. He had no notion of what was so humorous. It was unlike him to be so distracted. He must make an effort to concentrate on Margaux.

"That is a very fetching bonnet, Lady Margaux."

"Very pretty manners, Lord Vernon. Kind of you to join us at last." She gave a small laugh.

Drat! So she had noticed his inattentiveness. "Forgive me, my lady. My mind has been preoccupied. Shall we begin again?"

"Very well. But you need not ignore talking about her in front of me."

Rhys raised his eyebrows. "You certainly do not beat about the bush." He smiled.

"I find it makes things simpler. Should I not have said that?"

"Not at all. I am just unused to ladies speaking their mind. It is rather refreshing," he said reassuringly.

"Take comfort in knowing you will not ever have to wonder what I am thinking." She smiled. "My opinions seem to have trouble keeping to themselves."

"So clearly you know of my previous betrothal to Lady Beatrice."

She inclined her head in acknowledgement.

"Is there something you wish to ask?"

"Only it seems very soon to be courting again. No?" Realizing she had crossed the line, "Should I not have said that either? I do beg your pardon!"

She is bold, he thought. Her mother did warn me. She desires honesty? "Very well. I need an heir, and that requires a wife. I am no longer betrothed to Lady Beatrice, so now I am looking for a replacement. Does that bother you?"

She thought about this a while before answering, though utterly unruffled by his proclamation. "Not exactly. However, I do not wish to have a marriage of convenience. Friendship takes time to develop, does it not? So this will not be a quick decision for me."

Rhys looked away. He did not wish to involve feelings in the decision. He did not wish to risk his heart again, especially while it was still trying to heal. Margaux was wiser than he would have guessed for a diamond just out of the schoolroom. Most females would jump at the opportunity to marry one such as he, and most would not be given the choice.

63

She continued, "I hope you understand. I wanted to be open, should you not wish to expend your time on me."

"I would be honoured to know you better, Lady Margaux." What else could he say? "Shall we get down and take a turn about the park?"

She acquiesced, and they walked toward the Serpentine where it was less crowded. Beaujolais pulled out some bread to feed the birds.

"Jolie does this every day. Rain or shine. She loves to feed the animals," Margaux remarked.

Rhys could not help but think of Beatrice. There had been a previous occasion when they had been here to feed the ducks and one of them bit her. Another time they had been sitting on a bench and a bird had dropped a present on her bonnet. He laughed out loud. Beatrice just did not have luck with animals.

"Penny for your thoughts?" Margaux interrupted his reminiscing.

"I was just recalling another time when a friend was bitten feeding the birds here." Best to change the subject. "Are there any other things you enjoy?"

"I like to ride. I love to play games. I love to garden. Almost anything outdoors I like." She tossed another piece of bread to the geese hovering around them.

The exact opposite of Beatrice. *Stop thinking of her*, he chastised himself.

"And yourself? What does Lord Vernon love to do?"

"I suppose the usual things men fancy. Riding, boxing, fishing...nothing very original."

"What about the orphanage?"

"I do not think anyone actually likes orphanages."

She laughed appreciatively. "*Touché*. I will be more specific. How did you get involved with the orphanage? It seems quite the endeavour to undertake."

"It was not actually. There was a need. Lord Easton asked, and I helped." He shrugged his shoulders.

"You make it sound so simple."

"In my mind it is simple. If someone needs help and you can help, you help."

"I love children. I think it would be wonderful to be involved with the orphanage."

Rhys was pleased to hear she liked children. Hopefully, she would not protest about making them either. "Perhaps you will be able to visit with me in the future."

"I would enjoy that very much."

They walked on in silence for a few moments. Rhys noticed a crowd up ahead and Lady Lydia was at the centre. He stopped in his tracks. There was no one he could think of who he would rather see less than her. "Do you mind if we head back the other way?"

Lady Margaux noticed what made him stop. She was perceptive, thank heavens. She turned immediately with him and walked the other way without a word.

After they were far enough away from Lady Lydia's court, Margaux asked, "Care to talk about it? My brother would wish for me to remain silent at this moment."

Rhys could not help but laugh. "Nothing is taboo for you, is it? If you must know, Lady Lydia was one of Lady Beatrice's closest friends, if you could call it such. I am afraid I am not one of her ardent admirers."

"That is the way here. *Maman* has warned us of the society here. In France, it is not like this."

"Have you spent much time in France?" Rhys asked curiously.

"Yes, most of our childhood was spent there. Father wanted us to learn about his country as well, and when the war came it seemed best to leave for England."

"I spent some time in France before my father passed away, and then I had to return to take care of my family here."

"Please accept my condolences. Do you have any other family?" She stopped herself and lowered her head. "Forgive my impertinence. I often forget what is inappropriate to ask here."

"It is quite all right. It does not bother me to speak on it," Rhys replied. "I am guilty of several social blunders myself."

"Family is so important to me; I assume it is to others as well."

"I have a mother and sister who prefer to stay in the country, and a younger brother still up at university."

"Is your family upset about Lady Beatrice?"

Rhys barked a laugh. "I forgot to tell them. If my mother has not heard by now, there will be naught but rejoicing when she does hear."

Margaux looked at him with shock.

"Our fathers made the arrangement when we were young, despite our mothers' opposition. Our mothers were rivals their first Season, hence the opposition."

"Ah, I see."

"That's good, because I never did."

Dr. Craig visited Beatrice several times, but today he suggested a little change of scenery.

"That sounds like heaven. I am rather sick of staring at these walls," she said excitedly.

Dr. Craig laughed. "It sounds wonderful to be ordered to rest until you actually have to do it."

The doctor took her arm and walked her slowly down the stairs. He led her to a conservatory on the west side of the house. She sat down when they reached a bench, surprised at how fatigued she felt from a short walk after just a few days in bed. The conservatory was warm with sunshine and a fire in the hearth, and smelled fresh with the plants and flowers grown there throughout the year. The room had glass windows from floor to ceiling, providing a beautiful view of the mountains and the loch. After enjoying the beauty in silence for a few moments, Beatrice found herself curious about the handsome doctor.

"Did you always want to be a doctor?"

"I suppose. I am a second son, and I never fancied shooting people in the army, so I helped them after they were shot. I suppose I could have joined the church, but I prefer doing good works to preaching about them," he said contemplatively.

"What was the most interesting patient you ever had?" Beatrice found she was genuinely interested. Rarely had she had a conversation with someone new that was not trivial small talk.

"They are all interesting."

"Surely some more than others. The common cold cannot be as interesting as, as..."

"Being kicked in the face by a cow?" They both laughed.

"You must have seen some fascinating patients on the battlefield," she continued to probe.

"I always thought the most amazing part was that many of the soldiers dinna realize what had happened to them until much later."

"Why do you think that is?" she asked, intrigued.

"I suppose you could explain it as excitement or the fear of what was happening, being so close to death. Have you ever been frightened, your heart beating very fast and your breath catching?"

Beatrice nodded.

"You dinna notice it until after the fright has passed."

"Yes, that's exactly right," she recollected.

"I dinna do a verra eloquent job of explaining the medical phenomenon."

"I understand, though." She laughed.

"How about yourself? What do you think of Scotland? I ken you are not a native."

Beatrice was quiet. She averted her eyes and pretended to study the view.

"I beg your pardon. If you doona want to speak about your past, I willna ask again."

"No, it is just I do not have anything so honourable to say for myself." She paused. "As for Scotland, it is rather cold but beautiful."

"Aye, just wait for the spring. There is nowhere else that compares."

"Thank you, Doctor." She meant for not quizzing her about her past, but she could not speak the words.

"You're verra welcome. I thought you would enjoy a little change of scenery." He stood to escort her back.

"Yes, of course."

~

A week after her unfortunate experience with milking cows, Dr. Craig declared Beatrice fit again. She would have bruising for weeks, but she could do some tasks as long as she was not having pain or dizziness.

Beatrice never could have imagined how happy she would be to sweep and mop a floor, but she had never been confined to bed for more than a day or two with a cold before. She found she was better suited to the indoor work. She was helping clean the wing for the children, who were to start arriving later that week.

She had been scrubbing floors and making the new beds that had arrived. Her hands were raw and her back ached. She would never be the same again, but she found she did not mind so much. She sometimes thought about London and what it would be like to re-enter Society after this. She might be shunned, or everyone might act as if nothing had happened because of who she was.

She found herself thinking about Dr. Craig. He had been by several times during her week of convalescence, and he had even begun having conversations with her. She would not have been allowed to associate socially with a doctor before, and now he was the one highlight of her stay here. She even thought they might be friends; he had not shown any romantic interest in her. Although he might think of her as his social inferior, he did not act as such. It was a nice feeling to be appreciated for herself. Not for being the daughter of a duke; not for her dowry; for herself. It was an utterly new sensation.

She thought about Rhys, and her heart still ached. She needed to forget about him. Marriage to him was no longer an option. Life as she knew it before was no longer an option. Even if her father allowed her back, she would never be the same. She laughed. She would give anything to see her mother's face were she to see Beatrice now; she would dearly love to know how her father would explain her time in service! Under these circumstances, she would be lucky if she married a sheep farmer, she reflected as she scrubbed.

Miss Mary interrupted her daydreaming, "I never found scrubbing floors to be humorous." Miss Mary frowned reprovingly.

Beatrice stopped and sat back on her heels. "I am trying to make the best of things. Is something amiss?"

Miss Mary raised her eyebrows and looked around. "There does not appear to be. I thought you might welcome a break from cleaning. Do you know how to sew?"

"I know needlepoint fairly well, and I can mend."

"That is a start. I will show you the rest. We need to make some extra things for the children. We do not expect them to arrive with much."

Beatrice finally understood what it meant not to have much after having to wash her dresses every other day. She had helped make things for Society ladies' organizations, but there had never been faces or names, everything was just 'for the needy children'.

"What will the children be doing here?" Beatrice asked as they walked toward a sitting room. She had not seen any rocking horses or dolls such as had adorned her nursery as a child.

"We want this to be a place to learn as much as a safe place for the children to live, mostly basic letters and numbers. Is that something you think you could teach?" She gestured for Beatrice to sit and began pouring some tea.

Beatrice was in shock. She was to take tea with Miss Mary? Beatrice nodded. She believed she could teach letters and numbers. "Will they be able to play? I have not seen any toys."

"Naturally. We will make those as part of them learning to sew, or they will receive a gift for Christmas. We also plan to teach them skills so they can leave here and be able to find work. The older boys will be apprenticed to some of the villagers on the Master's land, and the girls will spend time with Cook or the housemaids so they have an opportunity to go into service."

"I think I could teach some to be a lady's maid, if you find that useful. I have little other skills I am afraid," Beatrice said.

"Perhaps. We will see where the children's interests lie."

Still no warmth from Miss Mary. Beatrice was thankful for the reprieve from housework and would be satisfied. "Have you heard anything from my family?" Beatrice ventured to ask. She thought her behaviour had been acceptable.

"No, I am afraid not."

Beatrice knew she should not be surprised, but she could not help the disappointment she felt. They finished their tea in silence. There was no point in elaborating on the fact that no one had cared enough to write to Beatrice, and she was grateful for the forbearance from Mary.

After setting aside the tea things, Miss Mary began teaching her to make some simple dresses for the girls.

"The new house-parents are due to arrive any day," Miss Mary said as she sewed.

"That will be a relief to you, I am sure," Beatrice said pleasantly. She knew she would welcome some help, and the children were not even there yet.

"The husband is a vicar. It will be nice to have clergy on the premises again. It has been a long time since we have had one in residence. And not a moment too soon."

Beatrice froze mid-stitch. She smiled as graciously as she could. Was Miss Mary insinuating she needed to confess and repent?

"Where did you attend services in London?" Miss Mary asked as she re-threaded a needle.

"At St. George's," Beatrice answered without looking up, noting the sudden religious turn of the conversation. Beatrice had known from the start that Mary disapproved of her, but she had done nothing singular enough to warrant a lecture.

"Your father did not tell me to preach you sermons, if that is what you were wondering," Miss Mary said astutely.

"I rather thought you might dwell upon the need for repentance," Beatrice responded honestly.

"No, but I will point out that the Lord does use some considerable mistakes for His good."

Beatrice held her tongue. She did not think her mistake of Biblical proportions.

"You are unsure of my meaning." She looked up at Beatrice. "You made a mistake. You have been given another chance. You are a fool if you do not learn from this."

CHAPTER 8

The day had finally come for the children to arrive. The trees were budding, and the snow had melted, signalling spring was in the air. Everyone bustled with anticipation, and the servants were finishing last-minute details. Beatrice's room had been moved to the wing where the children would reside. She was surprised to find it more like her room in England than the servant's quarters she had occupied since arriving. Addie continued to be her salvation in friendship, and in helping her learn to adjust to her new circumstances here. She could scarcely credit three months had passed since the ball that changed her life. She was still not comfortable with her situation here, but she had accepted it. Cook was gruff but had softened toward her, and Miss Mary was treating her civilly and more like an equal. That was all she dare hope for.

Beatrice was learning to be grateful for the small things, and she was no longer crying every day. Perhaps her father had even been right to send her here, for she did not know if she would have ever learned to appreciate anything if she had not been stripped of it all and forced to discover for herself. She thought back to the advice Addie had given her the first day. Not complaining had helped. She'd learned early on that acting as if she were superior would get her nowhere here.

The remainder of the servants still did not seem comfortable around her, and no one other than Addie bothered to talk to her. They spoke enough to convey messages, but they did not *talk* to her. She had been determined not to let them see her afraid of work. Beatrice still knew little about being a servant, but she did appreciate how hard the work was, and how lonely an existence that was devoid of friendships was.

The new house-parents had arrived. Vicar and Mrs. Millbanks were a young couple just married; a man of the cloth and a former governess. Beatrice could think of no one more appropriate to run an orphanage, had she had any experience with these things. Her first impressions of the couple were favourable. The vicar was a jolly, round fellow, who was a second son in a large family. Mrs. Millbanks was quiet and reserved, the eldest child of a widowed country squire, and she was experienced in managing children and households.

Beatrice had never been near children. She was the youngest in her family, and her brother had no children. But she had been a child once. Surely she could learn what to do, or the new house-mother would, hopefully, be kind enough to help. She certainly welcomed having another person at the priory with a genteel upbringing.

By that afternoon, several carriages full of children had arrived. Miss Mary warned Beatrice that the children would be wary of yet another new place, and concerned about how they would be treated. Many of the children had been tossed from place to place, had spent time on the streets or were rescued from abusive workhouses. She had seen the poor, dirty children on the streets in London and wondered how they did not freeze to death, but it was much colder here.

"One family of children will be arriving who have never been in an institution." Miss Mary continued as Beatrice watched children unload.

"Oh?" Beatrice's interest was piqued.

"Their father was a gentleman; both he and the mother were killed

73

in a carriage accident. The remaining relatives are unable to care for the children."

Or do not want to, Beatrice thought. *I understand not being wanted*, she reflected sadly.

"The adjustment will likely be most difficult for them."

"I will try to help as best I can." She could relate to a sudden change in station.

Miss Mary nodded. "Here is the family now. Why do you not take the children to their rooms and help them become situated?"

By dinner time, the priory was almost unrecognisable with the changes a houseful of children brought. The servants were taking on new duties as everyone tried to adjust to their new roles. The Douglas family that Beatrice was helping consisted of an eight-year-old boy, Seamus, a six-year-old girl, Catriona, and a two-year-old girl, Maili.

The boy kept his eyes downcast and only spoke in monosyllabic answers. Beatrice could understand that. He comprehended what was happening more than his sisters. The girls clung to her as their security. It was a strange feeling to have another person be dependent on you, to look up to you.

Dinner was simple fare, but good. The children were shown the rules about eating and cleaning up. The meal time was eerily quiet, save for the sounds of children devouring food. Beatrice looked around the table. Some of their faces showed sadness, some were pleasant, but some were devoid of emotion. Those faces were the ones that bothered her the most. She had never wanted for anything before, and even now she knew as long as she complied, she would be taken care of here. But, these little people had no such security; the thought sobered her.

There were no small babies, but there were two children under the age of two. Beatrice sat near one of them to help him eat. The little boy, Tobias, had already been served his food, which was mashed peas and carrots. In no time at all, he had managed to swirl them together into a disgusting concoction. He stirred and slopped his vegetables while turning the bread he was gumming into a wet paste that ran down his chin. Beatrice eyed the little man with dismay and wondered if she would be better off gathering eggs. She had yet to discover why people fawned over babies.

Addie was helping Maili to eat very neatly, Beatrice noticed. Addie looked over and said, "Spoon it in his mouth. He may not ken how."

Beatrice reached over to take the spoon; Tobias thought she was trying to steal it. He grabbed his spoon, which caused the bowl to go flying to the floor. Beatrice stood there bewildered, and Addie rushed over to calm the boy and reassure him as large tears rolled down his cheeks. "We will get ye another one, lad."

Beatrice retrieved another bowl of food for Tobias while Addie cleaned up the mess. She sat down to try again, and placed a spoonful of peas near his mouth. He eagerly took a bite. *This is how it is supposed to work,* she thought. She spooned up a mouthful of carrots and began to feed it to him, which he proceeded to spit back out in her face. "No, No!" she scolded. The other children were watching and giggled. Addie was trying not to laugh herself. Beatrice wiped the mush from her face.

"Ye might want to try a smaller dollop," Addie said, trying to be helpful.

She did not want to try anything, but she nodded and put a much smaller amount of peas on the spoon. This seemed to work well, and he finished them without further mishap. She lifted Tobias out of his seat when the meal was finished, and a foul smell began to waft toward her nose. Surely he did not just...he did. She dare not look down to see what remnants were left behind on her dress.

Addie realized what was happening and took pity on Beatrice. No, she had not changed a nappy before, and she was grateful to escape that one, from the smell of it.

Beatrice thought she was managing, with the minor exception of mashed peas and carrots, until bedtime arrived. The children needed to have their heads checked and have a bath. Simple enough. Beatrice would not mind a bath herself. Then she found she was in over her head, literally.

Addie was herding the other girls into the bathing room, while Beatrice was leading Catriona and Maili, as they hid behind her skirt. They could hear screams coming from behind the door.

"What on earth is happening?" Miss Mary and Mrs. Millbanks were supervising the head inspections, and Addie was starting the bathing line.

"Children who have never had a bath are sometimes terrified of water," Addie explained.

Never had a bath? Beatrice literally could not imagine.

"Check their heads for lice and nits, and if they are clean give 'em a bath. If ye find any, then tell Mrs. Millbanks and she can cut their hair and put some oil on it."

"L-l-lice?" That was what they meant by checking heads. She had not thought anything could be worse than never having had a bath.

"Ye want ter make sure it does not get in the beds an' spread. Check all over real close." Addie proceeded to demonstrate how to look at the scalp.

No, having lice in the bed would be worse. She looked at Catriona and Maili. They did not look like they should have lice. She looked carefully at the girls' hair and scalps, and thank God, no insects jumped out at her. She could not help compulsively itching, even though she had not seen any lice. Just knowing there might be some was enough.

At long last, the ordeal was over and she tucked Seamus, Catriona and Maili into bed and read them a story. She had never worked so hard in her entire life. How did people do this every day? She was asleep as soon as her head hit the pillow, and began dreaming about life before Scotland.

She was awoken to piercing screams. It took Beatrice a moment to comprehend what was happening, but she soon determined the screams were coming from the children's room across the hall. She threw off her covers and ran in to find Catriona upset and crying for her parents. Beatrice was completely at a loss as to what to do.

"What is the matter, Catriona?"

Sniff, sniff. "I had a dream about Mama and Papa."

"Do you wish to talk about it?" Beatrice sat on the bed and patted Catriona's arm.

"No." The little girl crawled up in Beatrice's lap and put her arms around her. Beatrice awkwardly patted the girl's back and struggled to find words to comfort the child. Nothing had prepared her for this moment, so she gave in and cuddled Catriona until they both fell asleep.

"You must go and retrieve her at once, Robert!" Wilhelmina, Duchess of Loring, exclaimed with as much vehemence as she was capable of gathering.

"Has something happened?" the Duke asked, concerned, for he was still worried he had made a grievous mistake with his daughter.

"Read this!" She waved the letter she had just received from Beatrice in his face.

He snapped it back and walked over toward a chair. He sat down before reading the script from his daughter. When he finished, he looked out of the window in thought.

"Something is dreadfully wrong! My daughter did not write that! That woman must have forced her to put these ridiculous words on paper, so we think everything is well!" She fell back onto the sofa and fanned herself. "Associating with doctors and orphans and all manner of riff-raff, as if it were acceptable! I thought she was to be at Vernon's hunting box with a gentlewoman. I told you this was unacceptable! She will never find a husband now, Robert."

"I agree, it does not sound like Beatrice, but it is certainly her handwriting." The Duke was uncertain of how to handle the situation. Beatrice had only been gone a few months. Could one change that quickly?

Nathaniel walked in the room. "Is something wrong with Bea?"

"Your mother is concerned about a letter we received from her. It does not sound like something your sister would write."

"May I see?" The Duke handed him the letter. Nathaniel perused the words from his sister with a slight laugh. "She must have been kicked in the head. It certainly sounds like a different Bea."

"Perhaps a trip to visit is in order. The letters I have received from Mary merely said she was making progress."

"I cannot believe you left her with that woman! My poor daughter! You must leave at once."

"I will have to put a few things in order first, Wilhelmina." He turned to speak with Nathaniel, dismissing her. She would have to be satisfied with that.

"How are you adjusting to England, my son? I have not seen much of you."

"I confess, I would rather be elsewhere. I feel decidedly out of place."

"Nonsense! Whatever put such a notion in your head?" The Duke looked up questioningly at his son.

"I am a soldier; it is in my blood now. Wellington sent word that Napoleon has escaped and has requested my return, with your permission, of course. With so many of our forces depleted with the American War, he is lacking for experience to mount a campaign against Boney."

"I see." This was not what the Duke wanted to hear. He son was only just home. He was not ready to lose him again.

"I cannot attend social functions gaily, knowing there is a war going on while my fellow soldiers fight for our freedom. I do not fit into Society any longer. I know Elinor has forgiven me, but if it pains me every time I see her, I can only imagine how she feels. She is happy with Easton and deserves to be rid of my presence."

"But you have a duty as my heir! To the people here!" The Duke could not believe what he was hearing.

Nathaniel shook his head. "I know this is difficult for you to understand, Father. Andrew is more than capable of helping should you need it, and you are hardly in your dotage."

"It is not right."

"Perhaps when Boney is defeated I will feel differently, but being here reminds me of everything I did wrong that I cannot make right. The wounds are still too fresh."

The Duke sat in silence. "I do not agree, but I will truly not have you here if your heart is there."

"Thank you, Father." The Duke stood to embrace his son, and tears gathered in his eyes. He could not help but feel he was losing him all over again.

CHAPTER 9

The London Season was in full swing. Rhys normally looked forward to this time of year, when he could dance with Beatrice as much as he chose, and he was not hounded by the matchmaking mamas and their young débutantes. There were many advantages to being betrothed. The rules were different this year, however, for he was merely courting Margaux, not betrothed to her. He found he was growing bored of the endless parade of dinners, balls and soirées. He needed to get on with his business before the Season ended. He went through the motions of alighting from his carriage, mounting the steps, greeting the hosts and being introduced.

Rhys scanned the ballroom, looking for the Ashbury family, so he could claim his two dances and be done with it. He should not be feeling this way. He had spent much time with Margaux. They had become friends; was that not what he had hoped for? His brow furrowed as he pondered his dilemma.

"Now that's not a face for the ballroom, Lord Vernon. Has something put you in a sour mood?" The infamous sultry voice spoke from behind him.

Lady Lydia. He pasted a smile on his face and turned around to greet her. "Ah, the lovely Lady Lydia." He bent over the proffered hand and kissed it, trying to avoid glancing at her charms, which were falling out of her fitted gown.

"Lord Vernon, it has been an age. I might think you were avoiding me, but I see you have been *préoccupé* with the enchanting Lady Margaux," she said as she glanced coquettishly up at him from beneath dark lashes.

"Just so." The less said the better.

"Have you heard from our mutual friend recently? It is a shame that no one speaks of her." She drew attention to her lips with a seductive pout.

"Indeed." For instance, she would not even say her name now as if it were taboo.

"Come to think on it, I have not seen her brother either," Lady Lydia continued, shamelessly hunting for more information.

Well, she would not receive any from him. He had no desire to continue this conversation or provide fodder for her gossiping pleasure. My, how refreshing Lady Margaux was compared to this! She would have asked what she wanted to know without playing games. Realizing he was unable to utter more than one-word responses to Lady Lydia, he excused himself to find more pleasant company.

"Do, please greet our friend if you see her. I would not want her to forget me," Lady Lydia called out to him as he walked off.

He would not allow Lady Lydia to affect him. He vowed he would work harder on enjoying his time with Lady Margaux. He spotted Andrew surrounded by the triplets. He made a mental note to discuss that with Andrew later. Rhys still had not been able to determine which triplet he favoured.

"Good evening, ladies, Abbott." Rhys bowed and greeted each sister individually. He secured a dance with each of them, feeling it might be prudent to take a turn with each of the sisters. He also noted there was little room left on any of their cards. Crowds of men swarmed nearby, probably hoping for an introduction.

"Has your evening been pleasant so far?" The orchestra began to strum the notes of the opening song, and Rhys held out his arm to escort Lady Margaux.

"It has been pleasant. And yours? I see you were accosted by Lady Lydia the moment you arrived," she replied.

Rhys had to smile. She did not miss anything. "I suppose I could not avoid her forever."

"I keep making myself unavailable to avoid an introduction." Lady Margaux smiled unrepentantly.

You had to appreciate her candour and unconventional nature, he thought, as the dance separated them.

"Do you leave for Scotland soon?" Lady Margaux asked when rejoined in the dance.

"I suppose that is approaching shortly. It had escaped my notice." He had tried to make it escape, anyway.

"There are many house parties being organized. Will you attend any?"

"Perhaps." They passed Andrew and the Lady Anjou during the next turn.

"You're having a house party?" Andrew asked.

"That sounds lovely!" Lady Anjou's eyes sparkled.

Rhys tried not to groan.

Lady Margaux giggled. "Will we be invited?"

"Of course." He smiled. A house party where Beatrice was staying was exactly what could *not* happen. He hoped she would be gone by the time he arrived, and the house party idea would be forgotten.

The next day Beatrice escorted the children to the drawing room to have examinations with Dr. Craig. She had not been able to find Seamus that morning. He was not at breakfast when she arrived, and she did not see him anywhere downstairs.

"Has anyone seen Seamus this morning?" She looked around the room searching for the boy.

All of the adults began to look around, and no one could recall seeing him.

"Where could he be?" She looked to Catriona,

"He was not in the room when we awoke." Catriona began to cry as she realized her brother was missing.

The Millbanks immediately organized a search through the house. "He is probably just confused and hiding." The clergyman in Vicar Millbanks tried to reassure everyone. "It is completely understandable in this situation."

Dr. Craig suggested a search party outdoors with people who knew the grounds well. "If he went outside, we may not have much time. Even though it is spring, the temperatures are still quite cold at night."

Beatrice felt her heart race. She was sure this was her fault. She had been asked to look after these children, and she had not made enough effort with Seamus. She assumed he needed time to himself and would talk when he felt better. How was she to know anything about eight-year-old boys?

Mrs. Millbanks quickly gathered the children into the great hall in order to keep them busy while the rest of the adults searched. Beatrice did not know the grounds well, but she could not bear the thought of Seamus being out there in the cold. She thought back to the hours she had spent in the cold coach on the way to the priory and shivered involuntarily. She frantically grabbed an extra blanket in case Seamus had gone out without a coat, and followed Dr. Craig's search party into the brisk spring air.

Beatrice had heard there was never a dull moment with children, and so far she felt that was a gross understatement. It had only been four-and-twenty hours since they had arrived, and she had had little time to think of anything else, let alone consider that a child might run away.

The men had split up to cover the estate grounds, and she and some of the servants searched around closer to the house. She had never been an outdoor person, and she certainly was not a boy, so she found it difficult to put herself in his place when she tried to contemplate where he could be.

Over two hours had passed, and the searchers had found no sign of him. There were so many places for him to become lost, especially in the darkness of night. She tried to recall places her brother and the boys had hidden around the estate growing up. She looked near the stables, behind the gardens, near any rock or good climbing tree she saw—to no avail. She fought back a wave of panic. She could hear her father's deep voice in her head telling her nothing good came from hysterics. Her own mother was proof of that.

The other adults began to come outside. That was not good news, for it meant they had not found him in the house. Miss Mary and Cook walked over to Dr. Craig and conversed. They shook their heads and looked about disapprovingly. Perhaps they were worried and assessing the situation, but Beatrice felt as if they were looking at her with blame. It was possibly her imagination, but she knew they expected no better from her. She ignored her desire to cower in shame and resolved to look harder.

She saw the men returning after completing the search of the grounds. Dr. Craig was suggesting a search party along the river toward the loch. Cook kept shaking her head disapprovingly, grumbling that they should have known this would happen.

Beatrice wandered away from the rest of the searchers, feeling self-conscious and responsible. She could not help berating herself for not knowing what to do. How would she tell those two little girls she had lost their brother, when they had just lost their parents and their home also? Beatrice's determination grew along with her desperation as time continued to pass with no sign of the boy.

She was chilled to the bone so she could not imagine how Seamus must feel. *Think harder. Think harder.* She thought back to her first day here when running away had seemed like the best option. She headed toward the drive thinking she would have followed the road to hail a lift to the nearest town. She knew how far and long the ride was to the nearest village, but would a child grasp that it was impossible on foot? The search party seemed to assume he would not have gone that way, but it made more and more sense to her as she went down the road.

Unfortunately, the snow had melted, so she was not able to see any footprints. She had walked at least a mile when she had to stop and rest. She was perspiring under her warm clothing, but she could still see her breath and her face burned with cold. She was cooling off quickly as she looked around for a place to sit and saw a large tree with a hollowed-out bottom. She walked closer and spotted a small pair of boots just under the overhang of the tree. Her heart began to race as she began to yell, "Seamus! Seamus!" She reached the boy and began to shake him, but there was no response.

Oh God! Oh God! What should I do? She prayed. She felt for him and tried to pull him out from under the tree. She could not see any breath coming from him, and his skin had a bluish hue. She realized she would either have to carry him back, or she would have to run and get help. She was afraid to leave him, so she had no choice but to carry him.

Beatrice wrapped him in the blanket she had brought. She had never fathomed how heavy a child was, especially a child who was dead weight. She struggled to lift him and barely managed. She wrapped him as tightly as she could and held him close to her, growing more distraught with each step, not knowing if she would have the strength to carry him the entire way.

It was slow going, and she despaired of reaching help in time. Her arms shook and ached from the burden, but at long last she made it back through the gates of the priory. Dr. Craig spotted her and ran over to relieve her of the boy.

"He's blue! Is he dead?" she asked, frightened that they were too late.

Dr. Craig felt for breath from the boy and tried to check his pulse. "He's alive, but near frozen. We need to get him warmed quickly." Beatrice was not reassured by Dr. Craig's reaction. They took off, running with the child to get him inside. Once there, Dr. Craig began to give orders for the supplies he needed to care for the child.

"We must warm him as quickly as possible," he instructed. "Fetch him some dry clothes and all the blankets you can find." The servants dispersed to find the items. He looked to Beatrice. "I have seen this in the army. He is fortunate he had his coat and boots on, but he must have been out there all night."

"Would a hot bath help? I know when I felt frozen after the trip here, a bath helped more than anything," Beatrice suggested.

"It probably would. We dinna have bath-tubs nor warm water on the battlefield."

Servants were sent to retrieve the bath. Once Seamus was in the water, he began to wake, but screamed with pain. He was pulled from the bath and wrapped heavily in blankets, and began to shake feverishly. Beatrice stood back and watched the flurry of activity, feeling wretched that the boy was suffering so due to her stupidity, but relieved that he had awoken. Not a word was said to her about fault in the matter, which was almost worse than a good tongue-lashing.

Cook brought in some steaming broth, worried and wanting to help. "I thought it might warm 'im from the inside," she said hopefully.

"Excellent, Cook. You read my mind," Dr. Craig said, pleased.

Cook beamed with pride. "Will he be all right?"

"I think so. We will have to see if he caught an inflammation of the lungs or not, but eight-year-old boys are strong and stubborn." This earned him a small scowl from Seamus through his chattering teeth, which Dr. Craig thought a very good sign.

Beatrice was exhausted, but she went to find Catriona and Maili to let them see that their brother was found. The girls entered the room, and Beatrice and Dr. Craig stood back to give them time.

"Why would you want to leave us? Were you looking for Mama and Papa?" Catriona asked. Maili just sucked her thumb and cuddled up on the bed next to her brother.

"I was going to find our family and come back for you," Seamus explained with a raspy voice.

Catriona thought about this but was not satisfied. "I thought we were here because there was no family left to care for us?" Seamus did not answer because his eyes were heavy, and he drifted off to sleep.

Beatrice's heart lurched as she listened to the siblings talk. She had a hard time understanding why she was here. How much more so for these children to try to comprehend.

Dr. Craig walked over and picked Maili up. "Your brother needs to rest now." Beatrice took Catriona's hand, and they led them out of the room.

"Does that mean my mama and papa are coming back?" Catriona asked.

"No, love. They live in heaven now." Dr. Craig said gently, and snuggled Maili to him.

"Will you be our mama and papa now?" The little girl looked from Beatrice to Dr. Craig.

Beatrice blushed. Dr. Craig knelt down to Catriona's level. "Your mama and papa dinna want to leave you, but God must have needed them. No one will ever replace your mama and papa, but we will all be here to help do the things they canna be here for."

"Do you promise?" she asked hopefully.

"I promise." He hugged both little girls tightly.

Beatrice watched with admiration, and wondered how she would be able to leave these children when the time came.

Beatrice decided to calm herself over a cup of tea in the parlour. The pale blue room was soothing to her in some way with its large windows and soft furniture. She had been through the gamut of emotions in a few hours and longed for some quiet. She even felt comforted by the sheep dotting the lawns. She would love reassurance that she was not a complete failure, but it seemed she was not fit for society or servitude. She was able to make a mull of everything she did. At least Seamus was safe and resting, and the girls were busy with their duties so she could indulge her pity and shame alone.

There was a slight knock on the door. Beatrice straightened herself subconsciously. Should she answer? Or should she remain silent?

Mrs. Millbanks poked her head around the door. "Would you mind some company? I quite understand if you want to be alone."

Beatrice gave a small smile in appreciation of the woman's astuteness. Something made her answer, "No, please join me," despite wanting to remain undisturbed.

"Would you care for tea?" Beatrice asked politely while motioning for Mrs. Millbanks to sit down.

The woman nodded. "Milk and two sugars, please. Thank you," she replied as Beatrice handed her the cup and saucer.

"Where do you originate from? Is it much different from here?"

Beatrice nodded. "Sussex. But we spend most of our time in London." She tried not to frown. She did not want to think about her old life at the moment. The other woman was saying everything that was nice, but nothing to the point. Just at this moment Beatrice did not feel like making small talk, but Mrs. Millbanks looked as though she wanted to say more.

"And yourself?" Beatrice managed to ask, her training as a lady returning out of habit.

"Lincolnshire. Mr. Millbanks and I were raised in the same village, and we welcomed the opportunity to marry and be together again here."

Beatrice smiled and tried not to think about her own situation. The woman was reaching out to her, and she had hoped for a friend.

Mrs. Millbanks continued, "I collect you have had a rough few days. It will improve."

"It does not signify," Beatrice waived the comment away as if it were not bothering her.

"No one blames you. It took me some time to know how children think and act, even though I was the eldest of four." She set her tea cup down. "The Lord knows I am far from faultless."

"Thank you. I suppose I am blaming myself, but that little boy could have died because of my ignorance." Beatrice did appreciate the reassurance, however, she was surprised it came from one so young as Mrs. Millbanks.

"You could not have known what he planned to do." She reached over and gave Beatrice's hand a squeeze of affection. As if reading her thoughts, "No one expects you to be perfect." She released Beatrice's hand. "Forgive me for speaking freely, but I remember how I felt when I took my first job as a governess. I thought you might feel the same."

Beatrice smiled appreciatively. Her words meant more than she would ever know.

CHAPTER 10

*A*ndrew strolled into Gentleman Jackson's boxing saloon, hoping he could find someone to spar with. He was restless and frustrated, and nothing seemed to help like good old-fashioned sweat and fists. He looked around for the Gentleman himself, but he was in the midst of a bout with someone. Someone rather skilled in the art of pugilism, by the looks of it, if he was holding his own with the Master. The man, stripped to advantage, was at least six feet of solid, chiselled muscle, fighting as if possessed.

"Enough!" Jackson held up his hands, exhausted from the exercise. His sparring partner turned around.

"Nathaniel?"

"Andrew. Care to join me? I am not quite ready to be finished." Nathaniel continued dancing around as if trying to expend his energy.

Jackson spoke up, "Better you than me, Abbott. I know when to cry off."

Andrew could think of no one else he would rather pummel at the moment. Vernon would be a close second, however. He hopped into the ring and bounced around to try to warm up. He threw a few practice jabs, then nodded to Nathaniel that he was ready.

A few swift punches from Nathaniel woke Andrew up quickly. "You've improved, cousin."

Andrew retaliated with several hits of his own. Boxing was how he dealt with the anger that was becoming increasingly hard to manage. For one, he had promised Elly that he would not take action against Nathaniel, pummelling him in the ring would have to do. For two, he was frustrated with Vernon. He did not understand how he could be so callous about courting Lady Margaux.

He threw a left hook that sent Nathaniel stumbling backward. "Nice chop," was Nathaniel's only reply. Both men were heaving and dripping with sweat.

"What's going on?" Nathaniel knew his cousin well, even though they were at odds since the revelation about Elly.

"Not one thing, but many little ones." Andrew shrugged.

Nathaniel nodded as if he knew he was one of the 'things'.

"And you?"

"You could hazard a guess."

"Elly," Andrew said it as a statement, not a guess.

"It was difficult to put one foot in front of the other when I was not reminded every day of what I had done. But being here just makes it more real again. I do not want her to have to see me every day."

"She has forgiven you."

"I do not deserve to be forgiven." Nathaniel looked away.

Andrew agreed completely. Suddenly, it dawned on him, Nathaniel was known as one of the fiercest, bravest fighters in the whole of the British Army. "That is why you fought like you did on the Peninsula. You wanted to die."

Nathaniel did not countenance the last remark. "I am going back."

"The Duke is allowing that?" Andrew asked, astonished.

Nathaniel nodded. "Since Napoleon escaped Elba, I am needed there. I do not have any purpose here," Nathaniel fidgeted with his gloves. "Fighting is how I occupy my time." He looked around him as if disgusted and shook his head. "It is deuced odd to walk around here as if none of it happened. I hear a noise that sounds like a rifle, and it's as if I am back there on the battlefield."

Andrew nodded. He had felt the same way many times. Society kept going as if the war was not happening, and when soldiers came home it was very difficult for them to readjust. Many of them had nightmares and shock from the atrocities they had seen and endured in the war. Many soldiers looked normal on the outside, but inside they were struggling. Those who were outwardly marred were often unable to find work and were shunned socially; men did not have emotional struggles.

Nathaniel had spent more time on the front lines than Andrew. He was a highly decorated and well respected commander who fought like he had nothing to lose, always side-by-side with his troops. Now Andrew understood why. Knowing his cousin had been disguised still did not make what happened to Elly less wrong, but knowing that Nathaniel was paying daily penance for hurting her made him soften his heart toward his cousin.

"Godspeed to you, Nathaniel." And he was astonished to find he truly meant the words. "I am sure to receive my marching orders soon as well."

"Take care of them for me," Nathaniel said sombrely.

Beatrice was sitting in the parlour with a group of older children at her feet, attempting to teach letters and their sounds. She was surprised how well they were learning, and how eager they were. Suddenly, one of the boys spotted a carriage coming up the drive. That's odd, Beatrice thought. No one ever visited in a carriage except the doctor, and he was already here visiting Seamus.

A few minutes later the parlour door opened, and Mrs. Millbanks came inside the door wide-eyed and looked toward Beatrice.

"Is something the matter, Mrs. Millbanks?" Beatrice looked up from the letter she had drawn on the slate.

"N-n-no. You have a visitor, Miss Beatrice," the house-mother managed to say.

"Very well. That will be all for now, children." This was met with a round of groans. Beatrice smiled. It pleased her that the children wanted to learn, and she was teaching them! She looked up and saw her father standing in the doorway behind Mrs. Millbanks, who looked terrified. Beatrice did not know whether to laugh or cry. She recovered her wits, as she noticed the children staring at the Duke, who was looking very ducal.

"Children, make your bows to his Grace, the Duke of Loring." She smiled to herself; she even sounded governess-ish.

The children looked at the Duke and nearly hit the floor with their bows and curtsies. They followed Mrs. Millbanks quietly out of the door, casting glances toward the Duke as they went. The door closed, and Beatrice and her father stared at one another wordlessly. She did not know what to say or how to act. She had very mixed emotions about seeing her father again.

"It appears your letter was written by you after all. Nathaniel said you must have taken a knock to the head," the Duke said good-humouredly.

Beatrice smiled. *If he only knew.* "Did Mama have the vapours?"

"Almost." He chuckled and held his arms open for her. She felt like a small child again for she wanted his affection and approval more than anything. She hesitated, but did go over and embrace her father. She understood better the children's need for her affection. She vowed to make more effort to show them.

"Is Mama well otherwise?"

"Your mother...well, your mother has become worse. It's as if she read that *Pride and Prejudice* book and decided Mrs. Bennett was competition." He let out a slight chuckle, then became serious again. "But she has taken a decided turn for the worse since Nathaniel left to rejoin Wellington."

"He left again?" Beatrice asked with disbelief.

The Duke nodded with visible pain written on his face. "Bonaparte escaped Elba, and Nathaniel felt like he could be more useful there. He...he did not feel comfortable in Society again."

"I am sorry, Father." She knew how much having Nathaniel back had meant to him.

"You seem to be doing an acceptable job with the children." The Duke changed the subject, uncomfortable with his emotions.

"Thank you, Father. I find I am enjoying them. I am not very skilled with most of the tasks given to me, but I am trying." Beatrice was proud. The children had made so much progress in a few short weeks.

"I can see that."

Beatrice indicated for him to sit down. "Would you care for some tea?"

"That would be most welcome. It was a long journey here."

Beatrice did not need to be told that. She knew exactly how long the journey was. "I will return shortly." She gave him a small curtsy and went to fetch the tea. She returned a few minutes later with the tea service, much to the surprise of the Duke.

"Are there no servants for that?"

"There are servants, but they are all busy adjusting to the extra work with the children here. Besides, Miss Mary says we all have to earn our keep here," she said matter-of-factly, as she poured him a cup of tea and added the milk as he preferred.

"Astonishing. What else have you learned here? What has happened to my daughter?" The Duke looked stupefied.

"You would not believe me if I told you. I am sure it would make for droll stories, though." She laughed. "I have gathered eggs, I plucked a chicken, I have milked a cow..." She thought some more. "I have changed infant napkins, I have mopped floors..."

"Enough! I did not send you here to be a common servant!"

"I assumed not, but I think it was the best thing that could have happened to me."

The Duke was clearly in shock. "Well, I am pleased you learned the lesson, regardless of the manner in which it occurred, but it is time for you to come home."

Beatrice set her cup down in her saucer. "I cannot do that, Father." Beatrice could not believe she had uttered those words, but she meant them.

"Pardon?"

"There are children here who need me. I think it would serve them ill were I to leave so soon." She stood and began to walk around, enthused to talk about her new life. "This family of children just lost their parents. Their father was a gentleman but did not leave enough behind to care for them. Miss Mary has left it to me to see to them, and they have grown rather attached to me."

"Perhaps I need to meet these incredible children who have convinced my daughter they need her more than her family."

Beatrice bit back a retort and simply nodded. If her father had told her he needed her before, this whole situation might not have happened. She would ignore the sarcasm in his statement for now. She knew he would adore the children when he met them.

Beatrice showed him to a room in the wing where the Master's quarters were. She had not been to this part of the house before. There was something about it that made her think of Rhys, with the sporting-themed paintings dressing the walls and the masculine-coloured furnishings. Strange, she thought. She had been so busy she had been able not to dwell on their severed relationship as much lately. Her heart still gave a twinge when she thought of him, but now her life had purpose and there were people here who depended on her.

She still cared what happened to him, however. "Father, is Rhys doing well?"

"I have not spoken to him lately, but when last I saw him he appeared well." He hesitated. "I must warn you, I believe a betrothal to one of the Ashbury girls is forthcoming."

"Oh?" Her heart contracted unbearably. "That's lovely for him. Wish them happy for me." She should have expected this, but somewhere in the recesses of her mind, she had hoped there might be a way that they could become reconciled—even though she knew that was unlikely after the way they had parted. She needed to be happy for him, and she did want for his happiness; she just had not expected the news to cause this much pain. Suddenly she needed to be alone.

"Dinner is at six. Shall I come and escort you to the dining room?"

"Yes, dear." She was afraid the Duke could see through her façade, so she smiled as best she could and walked quickly back to her room. She sat on the bed in silence, trying to sort through what had just happened. Maybe she truly had changed. Maybe loving someone meant letting them go if it meant they would be happier. But she could not believe how much she hurt inside. She lay her head down and bathed her pillow in tears until it was time for dinner.

~

Beatrice was amazed. Miss Mary had put together a formal dinner for their honoured guest. Beatrice had been hoping to have her father eat with the children. She looked down at her shabby clothing and laughed. A few months ago, she would have rather been caught dead than be seen in a dress a few years out of fashion. And, she might add, one that she had been working in the last few months. This was how her father had wanted it.

To his credit, he did not flinch when he opened his door to find her wearing the worn, outmoded garment.

"That reminds me," he turned to go back into his apartment, "your mother sent some things for you." He motioned toward a trunk of clothing. "My valet has readied a gown for you."

Beatrice thought long and hard about refusing him. He had been the one to send her here with only two dresses, and now he expected her to change when it was time for dinner?

"We do not have time, Father," she protested.

"The party will wait. Make haste." Beatrice obeyed and went into the dressing room to change, but she could not manage all of her tapes by herself. It had been months since she had worn a gown she could not fasten on her own. It was high-waisted, of coral and white striped sarsenet with lace trimming around the neck and sash. She peeked her head out of the dressing room.

"Father, would you ring for a maid to help me?"

The Duke checked his watch and shook his head. "I will help. That is less improper than my valet dressing you. He would expire on the spot."

Beatrice giggled. Her father had not been so informal with her in years. She turned and told him how to tie the tapes, and gave him a sincere smile. She checked her hair in the looking-glass. It was nothing fancy, but it would have to do. He held out his arm and led her to the dining room.

The small party was assembled in the drawing room, all wearing their evening attire. Dr. Craig was the only non-resident in attendance, looking as handsome as ever in his coat-tails. There was very little society in the local area, especially at this time of year when the Season was at its peak. The Millbanks were to dine with them, making a grand party of six. They openly stared at her as she walked in the room. Beatrice looked around the room and was about to make introductions when she noticed Miss Mary. Beatrice's mouth gaped at the sight before her.

Miss Mary looked like a grand lady. She probably did too, dressed in the first stare. Beatrice had never seen Miss Mary in anything other than drab grey. She looked years younger in her primrose crepe gown, and her hair dressed less severely with loose curls.

"Lady Mary. It is a pleasure to see you again." The Duke bowed formally over her hand.

Pardon?

"The pleasure is all mine, Duke." *Lady* Mary curtsied so low, Beatrice was surprised she was able to rise again. "Thank you for trusting me with your daughter. She has been a welcome addition to our home."

Mary was a lady? Beatrice nearly swooned. Was she hearing things? Lady Mary was being so sweet Beatrice thought she could be served for dessert. She felt as if she were a ghost watching someone who looked like her going through the motions of a dinner party. Introductions were made, and the Millbanks treated her and her father like royalty.

Why did it matter what their title was? She was no different yesterday than she was today. However, they were treating her differently. She was thankful that Mary had insisted on keeping her heritage quiet before. She had been able to act like herself—not like she was told to act—for the first time in her life. She hoped that would not change now. She did not ever want to revert to being the old Lady Beatrice.

The party made their way into the formal dining room, where portraits of horses and the hunt adorned the gold walls. The chandelier was glittering with candlelight, and the table was dressed as finely as any in London. Beatrice sat in between her father and Dr. Craig, though the table was oblong and the party small enough to make conversation possible by all.

Dr. Craig was speaking with the Duke about his work. Evidently, he had served with Nathaniel in the Peninsular Campaign. Dr. Craig did not seem surprised by her sudden change in station, and she hoped it would not affect their friendship, she reflected as she listened.

"Is this one of the children you were telling me about earlier, Bea?"

"Pardon?" She looked up. She had been completely detached from the conversation.

Dr. Craig saved her by saying, "I was telling your father how you rescued Seamus."

The Millbanks and Lady Mary all began to tell of her heroics.

"She searched diligently until she found him," Vicar Millbanks boasted.

"And she carried him all the way back," Lady Mary finished.

The Duke looked to her in amazement, seeing her in a new light. As if he were finally seeing the real Beatrice.

Dr. Craig added, "She even suggested a new treatment to me."

Beatrice coloured and looked down. She was unused to genuine praise.

"I did nothing; Dr. Craig was the one who saved him. He has come every day to look in on him, even after he was healed physically." She looked toward the doctor with admiration. "You take him on your rounds; you take him fishing; you have given him friendship and security."

"Seamus is easy to like. He seems genuinely interested in medicine. It is a shame; the poor lad should be in school now."

"I agree," Lady Mary chimed in, "perhaps we should speak to Lord..." she hesitated, "...the Master about sponsoring his education."

"I would be happy to sponsor him," the Duke offered.

Beatrice reached under the table and squeezed his hand gratefully. He gave it a squeeze back.

"How will that affect the little girls? If Lady Beatrice and Seamus leave, I think they will regress." Mrs. Millbanks spoke for the first time in the conversation.

"I do not have plans to leave," Beatrice said, to the surprise of everyone at the table. She continued, "I agree that the girls and I have become attached, and I would not leave them. At least, not now."

Dinner concluded, and the guests removed to the drawing room for tea. The Duke approached Beatrice. "Would you mind taking a walk in the garden?" He held out his arm for her, which she took. They walked in silence for a few minutes, taking in the fresh air and stars.

"I owe you an apology, Bea. I told you to go and change yourself, and you have. I just did not expect such a drastic transformation." He looked up as if to control his emotions. "I cannot help but feel like I have failed as a father." His voice quivered, "Nathaniel... when he was out of control, and I had to send him away, it was as if all of my dreams for him were shattered. I closed myself off to you." He paused. "Your mother and I have never quite agreed on how to bring you up, and I did not feel like fighting her any more when Nathaniel was gone."

Beatrice stayed silent. She had never seen this side of her father.

"When Nathaniel came back and I realized what had happened to Elinor...I snapped when I heard what you had said to her."

"I did not know, Father. I am sorry. I still should not have said what I did."

He nodded, trying to control his emotions. "Nathaniel said you did not know. Can you forgive me, Bea?"

She hugged him tightly and nodded.

"Will you please come home with me?"

She hesitated. "What is there to go back to? Rhys is engaged, and the children need me here. For the first time in my life, I feel worthy and useful." She sat on a bench and began to fidget with one of the branches on a bush. "The children do not know who I am, and they do not care."

"The girls can come home with us. They can be my wards. We can hire them a nurse, and you can see them every day."

"You would do that?" Beatrice could not believe what she was hearing. She thought about it and shook her head. "Thank you, Father, but I think for now it best to stay here. Perhaps when they have adjusted more and Seamus has gone to school."

The Duke was silent for a moment. "Do you think I could meet these children?"

Beatrice smiled. "I think that can be arranged."

The next morning, the Duke was already packed and ready to begin his journey back south when Beatrice ushered the children in to meet him.

"Seamus, Catriona, Maili Douglas, this is his Grace, the Duke of Loring."

The children bowed and curtsied as Beatrice had practiced with them, Maili wobbling a bit on the way up. She put her thumb in her mouth and tried her best to hold still. The Duke greeted each child and spoke with them individually.

"Seamus, would you care to attend school as you would have if your parents were still here?" Seamus nodded, but looked at the Duke wondering why he would ask such a thing. "If you promise to always do your best, I will help you go to school. Does that sound acceptable to you?"

Seamus looked away. "Thank you kindly, your Grace, but I am afraid I cannot accept your offer."

"Why ever not?"

Could the Duke not believe the boy would refuse such a generous gift?

"My sisters need me. I gave my word as a gentleman that I would not run away again, even though I was doing it to find our family."

"Ah. I understand. I promise Beatrice and I will look after your sisters, if that would make you feel better about leaving for school, and you may spend all of your holidays with them."

"Father," Beatrice gently warned under her breath.

"I am hoping your sisters will come and live at my house," the Duke persisted.

"Oh, can we? Can we really?" Catriona exclaimed. She looked to Beatrice for confirmation.

How dare he put her in this position! "Maybe one day soon. I think it best if we stay here a little while longer. At least until Seamus is ready to go to school in the autumn."

The little girl tried not to look disappointed and nodded her head.

"Run along now and do your lessons so I can say goodbye to my father."

The children left out the door, and Beatrice turned with her hands on her hips. "That was a fine trick, Father."

He smiled unrepentantly and threw his hands up. "I am used to getting my way."

He handed her a purse of money. She looked at him questioningly. "If you choose to return on your own, post with a maid, or send word, I will come as soon as I may even though this feels like the ends of the earth!"

She thought it strange he would now be concerned with propriety, but chose not to question it. "Thank you, Father."

He wrapped her in a paternal hug and squeezed a little tighter. "Whatever am I to tell your mother?"

She did not answer. She did not want to think about her mother's reaction. She felt a tinge of guilt for leaving him to deal with her, but she knew deep down she was making the right decision.

"Goodbye, my dear."

CHAPTER 11

*L*ady Ashbury was hosting an afternoon garden party, à la Grecque, and togas were the favoured costume of the day, along with some under-dressed Greek statues. The Ashbury property bordered the Thames, and many of the guests chose to arrive by sculls. The extensive gardens were decorated with statues and topiaries; lawn chess, tennis and pall-mall were available for those capable of wielding a giant pawn, racquet or mallet in a toga.

Fountains flowed with wine, and tables covered with native Grecian fare were in abundance throughout the gardens. String quartets added to the ambience. It was the perfect place for a proposal, Rhys reflected. He thought Lady Margaux would agree by now. She had not discouraged his court, but something inside was keeping him from moving forward. Perhaps the deranged part of his brain was hoping the Duke would bring Beatrice back with him, and he would wake up from this unending nightmare.

"There you are, Lord Vernon. We were hoping you would attend today." Lady Ashbury held out her hand to him.

"Miss one of Lady Ashbury's exclusive parties?" He playfully feigned offence.

She reprimanded him with a tap of her fan but preened under the praise nevertheless.

Lady Ashbury saw her daughters and waved them over. The triplets joined them, and after the usual trivialities, Lady Anjou spoke up, "Is it true that Lord Fairmont went back to the Continent? We have not seen him for weeks but just heard the news."

"It is hard to believe the Duke allowed him to go willingly," Lady Ashbury commented.

Rhys remained quiet. It was still not known what had occurred between Nathaniel and Elinor, and they hoped to keep it that way for everyone's sake. Although the heir to a dukedom was permitted almost any sin, the effect on Elly would be devastating.

"Apparently Lord Wellington was able to convince him," Lady Beaujolais stated pragmatically.

"I am sure the Duchess is beside herself. Perhaps they will bring Lady Beatrice back from the sick relatives she has been visiting," Lady Ashbury said thoughtfully.

A polite way to avoid saying Rhys was jilted.

Sick relatives, he scoffed. It was gossiped about in closed parlours of course, but no one dare speak ill of the Duke's daughter openly. Rhys had received some scornful looks from the high sticklers, but he knew the truth and brushed them off. He had not been cut by Beatrice's family, so everyone assumed he was the wronged party. He felt wronged. Rhys was lost in thought, not paying attention to the ladies' speculations.

They were still gossiping, though not with malice, by the time he rejoined the conversation. "It's true. I spoke with her mother yesterday. They have no idea where she is." Lady Ashbury seemed genuinely concerned.

"I never cared for her myself, but I do not wish her ill," Lady Margaux said frankly.

Were they still speaking of Beatrice?

"Poor Lady Lydia," Lady Anjou said sympathetically.

Ah. Rhys had little doubt that Lady Lydia knew exactly what she was about. Though it was possible she had got herself in over her head, he doubted her act was pure naiveté. She was on the arm of a new beau every week. He suspected they would hear of Lydia's elopement to Gretna within the week. He had no desire to listen to speculation on Lady Lydia's entanglements, and it was time to move on with his plan.

"Lady Margaux, would you care to join me for a stroll through the garden?"

Lady Ashbury smiled hopefully.

"Of course, as long as we do not miss the pall-mall tournament. Or do you prefer chess or shuttlecock? You look more like a chess player." She looked him over thoughtfully.

"I like them all?" Rhys shrugged and held out his arm to escort her away from the others.

"You are being diplomatic again. If you ever find yourself in need of work, you should consider the profession."

"Duly noted. However, I was being honest. I do like all of the games."

"Very well. I am the family champion three years running, and I do not care to lose."

Who would have thought Lady Margaux had such a competitive streak?

"Do not look at me thus! When you are the youngest of four, you must take the victories where you can find them."

They strolled on through the garden. Rhys could not bring himself to propose as he fingered the ring he had always intended to give Beatrice in his pocket. Margaux felt more like one of his school chums than a prospective wife. He chastised himself. He wanted to like the person he married after all. Just as he was building up the courage, Margaux brought up Scotland.

"So when is your house party to start?"

"Pardon?" Please let her be jesting.

"My sisters and I are all excited to visit the orphanage. We used to visit one in France. We are hoping that after we visit yours, we can convince our father to open another. He was very interested after talking to Lord Easton. He wants to understand how this new approach works."

"You refer to educating the children?" Rhys asked.

Lady Margaux nodded.

Rhys continued, "It is not so unusual. Instead of simply feeding the children and having them do jobs, we teach them skills so they can make their own way when they are ready to leave."

"That is why we are so delighted to see your orphanage. The ones we have been to before are depressing. The children do not laugh. They seem to have no purpose but work and are sickly. The people have no expectations of them save labour, and treat them as only another mouth to feed," Lady Margaux explained passionately.

Rhys was holding his breath. How could he refuse? He had to pray that the Duke was bringing Beatrice home, but the letter received merely indicated a visit. He could not fathom the disaster it would be for them to all be there together. He was sure Beatrice knew he owned the priory by now. If his aunt had not relayed the information, he felt sure Beatrice would have deduced as much. Besides that, he did not trust himself around her yet.

"So the party is still on?" Margaux asked, interrupting his ponderings.

Rhys smiled. "I did not have any formal house party planned."

Her face bore the look of utter disappointment. Rhys was well aware that her usual perceptiveness was failing at the moment he needed it most.

"But I think it permissible to have a small gathering. With the orphanage just opened, I would not want to overwhelm the children or my servants."

"Of course not! We will bring the staff for ourselves. They will not even know we are there."

Perhaps not, but he would. "Very well. You have persuaded me." He was addle-brained! Why had he consented to this madness?

"You are too good! When can we leave?" She gave his arm a squeeze.

He had to fight back the laughter of the insane welling up inside him. "I agreed to help Easton transport the children to his new boarding school, but when that is complete. I will send word to warn the staff."

"I cannot wait to inform *Maman* and the girls!" She began walking back to find her mother, and Rhys punched the tree next to him.

Rare was the situation where the Duke did not see the immediate solution to; he pondered the conundrum of Beatrice most of the journey back to London. The Season was just concluding, and most of Society would be heading to their country houses for the summer. He felt like he should warn Vernon about Beatrice's continued residence, before Vernon went to the priory for his annual visit. Neither of them had considered the consequences of having her at Vernon's property indefinitely, and the Duke certainly never anticipated the current situation. The orphanage was not as far removed from the great house as he expected; rather, it was part of it. There would be no way for them to completely avoid one another. He knew Vernon had cared deeply for Beatrice at one time, and it was obvious that she still cared for him.

The Duke rapped on the ceiling of the carriage and instructed the driver to stop by Vernon's town-house before going home. When the Duke arrived, Vernon had just returned from a garden party. He looked as harried as the Duke felt.

"Sir. To what do I owe the honour?" The Duke shook his hand instead of the customary bow. "I confess I was surprised to receive the news of your trip. Are you just returned?"

"I apologize for thrusting upon you in such a fashion. I have only now driven into town."

"Not at all. I trust you were well received at the priory. It is a bloody long way though. Care for a drink?" Vernon gestured for him to take a seat.

The Duke nodded. Vernon poured two glasses of sherry and

handed one to the Duke. He was unsure how best to tell Vernon. "Beatrice refused to return with me."

The Duke noticed Vernon had to stop himself from spilling his drink. "I do not understand." Vernon managed to speak with tolerable composure considering the staggering intelligence imparted to him.

"I own, I almost did not recognize my own daughter."

"Has she fallen ill?" Vernon asked worriedly.

The Duke shook his head. "You misunderstand me. I found her in perfect health." Vernon visibly relaxed. "Who would have presumed she could change so much, so quickly?"

"Who indeed?"

"She has grown rather attached to a family of children recently orphaned, a gentleman's children. I offered to bring them here and to put the boy through school, but she remained adamant in her refusal to leave."

Vernon was speechless.

"I admit I was frustrated, yet I am proud of her." The Duke rose to leave. "I was persuaded you would wish to know the circumstances if you wished to curtail your usual summer visit."

"I am much obliged." Vernon looked away, distracted.

The Duke made to take his leave and remembered something, "Oh, I informed her you were betrothed to one of the Ashbury girls." Vernon looked up, surprised. "She said to wish you happy."

The Duke missed Vernon's look of despair.

Easton and Elinor travelled in the carriage the short distance to the new boarding school they had built on the property in Sussex. The school would house many of the orphans they had taken in and teach them a trade. This would open up more room in the London orphanage to rescue more children. They were constructing two more schools on other estates in England, in addition to the one Vernon had opened on his property. Buffy and Josie, Easton and

Elinor's valet and maid, had married and volunteered to be the new house-parents here.

Dr. McGinnis had been teaching Elinor and Josie about medicine, and they were going to teach the trade to the students who desired to work in hospitals or as army medics. Buffy was a wizard with horses, and he would train boys to be grooms or postilions while helping Easton with the estate's prized breeding stables.

Easton and Elinor pulled up in front of the new school as Sir Charles came out to greet them with Susie in tow. She was one of the girls from the orphanage with whom Easton had formed a special bond. She immediately ran to Easton and he swung her up in the air. "Papa Adam!" she cried, hugging him and giving him a wet kiss on the cheek.

"There's my girl!"

"Have the children arrived yet?" Elinor inquired, hoping they had made it in time.

"Not yet. But Susie and Adam are keeping the Earl and me on our toes." He chuckled, and it was obvious the two new additions to the family were melting their grandfathers' hearts. They entered into the parlour to find Adam, the little boy from the orphanage who none of them could resist, curled up on the Earl's lap with a story.

Josie bustled in and ran over to hastily greet Easton and Elinor. She bobbed a quick curtsy, then hurried back to the kitchen to remove biscuits from the oven. Elinor made a step to go and assist her and was immediately stopped by her father, Easton, and a look from the Earl. She sighed, knowing it was useless to argue with all three of them together and availed herself of the nearest chair. Her feet were immediately swept atop a stool. If she were not feeling so exhausted from being with child, she would have thought herself a queen.

The sound of carriages approaching grew, and everyone but the Earl rose to their feet to greet the newcomers. The Earl had improved immensely under the watchful eye and happiness of his family, but walking was still quite taxing. The door to the first carriage swung open and Andrew climbed out first, looking harried, and was rapidly followed by several children.

"If this was your plot to get me leg-shackled, I am afraid it is not having the desired effect." They all laughed. "I mean, they are charming—in limited doses," he said nodding to the children.

"You will feel differently when they are your own," Sir Charles tried to point out jestingly.

"Do not bet on it," Andrew mumbled none too quietly under his breath.

Two other carriages full of children followed in rapid succession, and each chaperone who alighted first was equally exasperated. Andrew led Vernon straight toward the library looking for a drink. Buffy went to look for his wife.

"You owe us, Easton," Vernon mumbled as he walked by, cravat askew and hair dishevelled. Andrew winked as he passed Easton and Elinor.

"I am much obliged. I would have been happy to retrieve the children if you would have stayed here with Elinor."

Both of them looked at the increasing Elinor and shuddered. Andrew leaned over to give his little sister a kiss, making a great show of avoiding her large belly before continuing on the way for a drink. Laughter followed them all the way out.

That evening, after the new arrivals had been settled in, and after Susie and Adam had been tucked in their beds, Elinor lay on the sofa as Easton rubbed her swollen feet. Eyes closed, she smiled blissfully.

"Is all well in your world now, Mrs. Trowbridge?" He smiled up at her.

"Why yes, Mr. Trowbridge. I cannot think of a more perfect day." She relaxed with the magic he was performing on her feet. "I do love a happy ending."

"I hope you mean for yourself as well."

Elinor's eyes popped open at that comment. "I cannot believe you must ask. I never thought any of this possible. You have given me a new life. I thought I knew better, but you have given me more than I could have ever dreamed of." She smiled at him with all the love in her heart. He placed his hand on their child growing inside her, and the child kicked his hand.

"It feels like little Trowbridge is full grown by the feel of that kick." He laughed in astonishment.

"It feels like little Trowbridge is full grown by the feel of my stomach, my ankles, my chins…"

"You still have a few months to go!" Easton exclaimed.

"I blame you entirely. My side of the family does not propagate giants," Elinor said haughtily.

"We do not have giants, merely triplets." Easton grinned mischievously.

After Andrew and Rhys had recovered from their child-transporting adventures, they rode ahead to the priory. Rhys wanted to greet the children and speak to Beatrice before the Ashburys arrived.

The two rode long and hard, only stopping briefly for meals and changes of horses the first day. They journeyed in comfortable silence, absorbed in their own thoughts. Andrew came along for moral support, although he was, as yet, blissfully unaware of it. Rhys needed to compose himself and determine how to resolve this self-made disaster. Andrew understood and did not ask unnecessary questions. For instance, he had not even asked him why he was coming all the way to Scotland with him. He likely assumed it was to even out numbers at the dinner table.

Long journeys could be conducive to deep thinking, but Rhys had reached a point non plus. Ignoring the problem would not make it cease to exist. After racking his brain for every possible solution, Rhys decided he best warn Andrew before they arrived since they had already passed Gretna. Andrew did know Beatrice very well, after all.

"Andrew?" They slowed their horses to a trot and Rhys pulled beside Andrew. "I think it time to make a confession as to why I asked you along."

"Because you cannot bear to be without me?" Andrew looked at him in mock seriousness, cocking one of his expressive eyebrows.

"Precisely," Rhys retorted.

"I knew it. I dare say you wish to leg-shackle me to one of the other triplets."

"I am not interfering with your amorous pursuits."

"Wise man."

"Beatrice is at the priory."

Andrew said not a word, and immediately pulled his horse to a stop. He dramatically turned around to head in the other direction. Rhys also stopped his horse, but did not turn.

They sat there for several minutes, both facing opposite directions, motionless except for the stomping from their restless horses. Rhys waited for Andrew to digest the situation. He knew Andrew was merely making a point.

Finally, Andrew spoke, "I should draw your cork. Wait, no, first I need to know, do you have a wish to die? Uncle said he had sent her north to a..." Andrew slapped the side of his leg. "Vernon!" Andrew growled as he put two and two together.

"Call me whatever you like, but turn around," Rhys pleaded.

"I must be dicked in the nob. You do not deserve me," Andrew said as he turned the horse back around. He made expressive gestures, while mumbling to himself about idiots, lunacy and abuse of friends, but continued on with Rhys.

They both mulled over the situation and neither seemed to know quite how to handle the impending disaster. "There is nothing for it but to send Bea away before the Ashburys arrive. I do not care how reformed Bea is; when Lady Margaux is dancing around on your arm, Bea will come unhinged. Or, Lady Margaux will see how you still look at Bea and her claws will come out. Either way equals doom," Andrew said decidedly.

"I do not care to hear this." Rhys shook his head, pretending not to listen.

Andrew, not to be deterred, kept on, "Ladies are territorial, and when they fight, they are ruthless. They make Salamanca look like child's play." They both shuddered, recalling one of the fiercest battles they had been a part of in the Peninsular War. "I have it! Set up a mill and charge admission. My money is on Bea."

Rhys ignored Andrew, but he knew he was right. He had seen women unleash their venom first-hand in Society. "But why would Bea care? She chose this! She was indifferent to me the whole of last year."

"Pure faradiddle."

"And when she refused to talk to me the day she left? She had ample opportunity to explain."

"Never attempt to understand a woman." The men simultaneously spurred their horses to a gallop.

CHAPTER 12

*S*ince the weather had grown warmer, and the sun shone early, Beatrice had started taking morning walks before breaking her fast. Breakfast had always been in bed before, and never before noon. Now, she purposefully rose early before the children to have some time alone. She had never found enjoyment in the outdoors before, but now it was essential to her sanity. She walked toward the river and perched on a rock. She reflected on her circumstances as she watched the water flow down the mountain into the loch. Dr. Craig was correct: Scotland was incomparable in the summer.

Beatrice revelled in the peace here, but she knew she must return to London soon. The girls were adjusting wonderfully. Catriona's nightmares were occurring less often, and Seamus was blooming under Dr. Craig's attentions. Beatrice could defy her father and stay indefinitely, but that was not what she wished when she finally felt their relationship had promise. However, before she could go back, she would have to define what she did want, and learn to stay within those boundaries with her parents.

Everything was muddled when she tried to envision her future.

Where did she belong now? When Lady Mary told her the house party was due to arrive, she was startled to realize she had not even missed the Season. She felt caught between two worlds—unsure if she would ever belong there again, but not quite belonging here either. Lady Mary had told her the Master was bringing his prospective bride. Beatrice had envisioned the Master to be older like her father, so she was surprised to hear he was a bachelor.

Returning to London meant seeing Rhys and his new bride. *It should have been my wedding this summer*, she thought sadly. Would her parents try to attach her to someone else soon? Very likely. Making a match was what young ladies did. The thought of marrying an old man in his dotage sprang into her mind; she was repulsed by the thought. Perhaps staying here might be the answer after all.

Beatrice made her way back up the slope to the house. Dr. Craig was dismounting from his gig and escorted her from the stables.

"Guid morning. You are about early." He fell into step beside her.

"I have found it is the only time I am assured of quiet. Is someone ill?" Beatrice asked, concerned. He was here earlier than usual.

"No, only collecting Seamus for my rounds." He smiled at her reassuringly. "Would you walk a little with me?"

"Of course, though I must return to help with breakfast."

They strolled toward the garden near the conservatory where he had brought her the day she was recuperating from her injury. He led her down a path among the lilies that were in full bloom.

"Do you mean to return to London soon?"

Beatrice hesitated. "I am undecided. I do not know what is there for me any more, but I am considering. It would be a marvellous opportunity for the children."

"But, they are happy and thriving here." He looked away before turning back to her. "I would be pleased if you would consider staying."

"You would?" She looked up and searched his eyes. Was he saying what she thought he was?

"I know I am not a wealthy lord, but I live verra comfortably and..."

She stopped him with her hand. "Those things do not matter to me any more. I have learned to be happy, even content here." She looked down and fidgeted with a button on her gown. When she looked up, Dr. Craig leaned in and planted a soft kiss on her lips.

She started to speak, but he placed a finger over her lips. "Shh. I have surprised you. Take some time to think about it. I doona know why you were sent here, but I doona care. I ken what you are now."

He squeezed her hand and walked her towards the house. It was not at all expected, but was not unpleasant. Maybe she should consider his offer. After all, it would be someone of her choosing, not her parents. Would her father consent? They seemed to get along famously when he was here. Her mother would think it a ruinous occasion and a most disadvantageous match. She could practically hear the words: *shocking mésalliance.*

They stopped shy of the house. "I am flattered, Dr. Craig. I will consider your offer."

"Please call me Gavin."

"Gavin." She repeated his name tentatively. He reached down and gave her another quick brush of the lips.

"I see you have not wasted any time, Beatrice," Rhys said stiffly, as he and Andrew walked out of the stables and spied her embracing Dr. Craig.

Beatrice startled and jumped back from Dr. Craig. "Rhys?"

"I see you were not expecting me."

"Should I have done?" Beatrice asked, eyeing him in astonishment.

"I sent word to Aunt Mary weeks ago," he replied coldly.

"Aunt Mary?" He was the Master?

Andrew greeted Beatrice, "Hello, Bea, we will leave you two to become...reacquainted," he hinted strongly toward the doctor.

"Is that all right with you, Beatrice?" Dr. Craig asked protectively. She nodded, too shocked to answer him. The two men went into the house.

Beatrice stood staring at Rhys. So he was the Master, and he was here. So many details began to swirl in her head. "Is this some kind of cruel joke?" She was becoming angry as the pieces of the puzzle began to fit together. "*You* were the family friend. *You* were the one who sent me here to be a common servant, and now you bring your bride here to remind me of my new place? Shall I serve the two of you at your table so you can show her what I am to you now?"

Lady Mary opened the door. "Lady Beatrice," she said with a warning tone in her voice.

Beatrice turned and saw Lady Mary. "Were you all in this together? Were you deliberately deceiving me? What fun you must have had putting me in my rightful place!"

At this undignified speech, Beatrice turned and hastened away as fast as she could, trying to fight off tears.

"Bea! Wait!"

Mary put out a hand to stop her nephew as he was about to go after her.

"Let her go. She needs time."

Her first thought when she saw Rhys was to throw herself into his arms; he was looking more handsome than ever after his ride. But then the reality of the situation overwhelmed her. Rhys was the elusive Master she had been hearing about for months. Was this just a game to him? She stumbled as she ran down the slope. Perhaps she was not so reformed as she thought herself. Seeing him brought all of the hurt back.

Beatrice tried not to pity herself, but she felt abandoned and humiliated. It struck her—*this must be how Elly felt when I said that to her at the ball.* It was hard to compare her situation to Elly's violation, but she did sympathize. She had not realized the acute anguish she would feel at seeing Rhys again. One of the blessings about her time here was it had kept her too busy to dwell on him for long.

She wandered on down the path until her feet hurt. She had never walked all the way to the loch before. Her tears had run dry, but she was not ready to face anyone yet. She found a place to sit and try to sort through her feelings. She knew she could not stay at the priory.

She could not bear to watch Rhys with someone else, or to be living at his house playing second fiddle to his wife. She would ask Lady Mary to arrange for her and the girls to leave. If Seamus wanted to stay with Dr. Craig until school started, then so be it. She would simply avoid the house party until she left, and hope that would not be too long.

Beatrice noticed Andrew out on the pier with some of the children fishing. Fishing was one of Rhys's favourite things to do, she reflected. The boys were so excited whenever they were taken on special outings. She was startled when she became aware of how much she would miss the children. She watched the boys fish awhile, and then she walked around the loch until she felt like it was late enough to return without being noticed.

Rhys watched Beatrice hurry away and his heart sank. This was not how he had envisioned seeing her again. His aunt tried to comfort him, but he brushed past her and went into the library. Would the torture never end? When he saw the doctor embracing Beatrice, he wanted to strangle him. At least he knew he had not been mistaken about her indifference, but it pained him just as much now as it had then. He heard the carriages arriving for the house party. He groaned. So soon? He needed time to compose himself. Why had he allowed this to happen? He would have to tell Lady Margaux that Beatrice was here. That was not a conversation he looked forward to, but he could procrastinate no longer. He needed to seek out Beatrice and apologize, but that would have to wait.

He walked outside to greet the Ashburys. "Welcome to Alberfoyle Priory," Rhys said more jovially than he felt.

The girls alighted from the carriage and looked around in awe. They were all dressed in matching travelling frocks and bonnets.

"Lord Vernon, it's beautiful here!" Lady Beaujolais remarked.

"I see why you make it a priority to visit here every year," Lord Ashbury said, pleased with the surroundings.

"Please come in and rest from your journey. Lady Mary will show you to your rooms, and I will be happy to give you a tour once you are settled. Mr. Abbott took some of the children fishing. If he had known you would arrive this soon I am sure he would have refrained."

"That sounds delightful! I am thrilled to know you allow the children some leisure time," Lady Ashbury said as they entered the house.

"We try to be the antithesis of a workhouse." Rhys smiled. "I hope you are not too weary for pall-mall. We promised the children a game after tea."

"Never!" Lady Margaux said with unimpaired cheerfulness.

"You had better tell Margaux to be gentle with the children," Lady Anjou added playfully as they made their way into the house.

The Ashburys were shown to their rooms and promised to return for a tour of the orphanage before tea.

Rhys normally would have enjoyed giving a tour of his beloved priory and even playing pall-mall with the children. But, when informed that Beatrice had still not returned from their earlier confrontation, his nerves were wracked with pain. He should have had the foresight to perceive she would be cross about the situation. He never anticipated she would have still been here. Nor could he have foreseen she would not surmise he was the owner when he told his aunt not to mention the fact at first.

He hit his ball with a bit more force than he intended.

"Easy, Vernon. The ball is not the enemy," Andrew teased. The children were impressed as the ball sailed across the lawn. "Care to talk about it?"

"What else is there to say?" He shook his head and then stepped up to help one of the children with their form. "I am a royal mess? I am jealous? I am pathetic?"

"I will not argue with you on that head," Andrew said helpfully.

"Seeing her today only reinforces what I felt all Season—she is indifferent to me in that regard." He slammed his mallet down in frustration. "Coming here was a mistake. This is not fair to Lady

Margaux, but she made it deuced impossible for me to refuse this party."

"Well, here we are, so you had best come up with a solution." Andrew was not one to mince words.

"I plan to be honest with her, and will naturally honour the under-standing with her."

Rhys felt a tug at his jacket, "Master, Master! Lady Bo-zho-lay's ball went in the water!"

Rhys knelt down to be eye-level with the little boy, chuckling at the pronunciation of her name. "Does she need my help?"

The boy nodded his head vigorously.

Rhys looked at Andrew, "Mr. Abbott, should we go offer our services to the ladies?"

"Of course. Always obliged to help a damsel in distress."

"Do not tell, but I saw Lady An-jew hit the ball in the water," the boy confided to the men as they walked. "Lady Mar-go said not to tell anybody."

Rhys and Andrew mutually looked at each other behind the boy's back and shrugged.

"Let me know how being honest works for you, Vernon," Andrew retorted.

Beatrice managed to avoid the party guests. She assumed they were still at dinner. She did not have anything particular against the Ashburys, but her feelings were too raw to sit through an entire evening pretending to enjoy trivial small talk, and she was not ready to face Dr. Craig or Rhys. She entered the house through the kitchen and received a worried tongue-lashing from Cook. She had intended to sneak up to her room and tuck the children in, but she could not help herself from listening a few moments from the hallway. A talent the Duchess had fostered long ago. She stopped and leaned against the wall.

"Lady Beatrice has been living here the whole time?" Lady

Ashbury asked with surprise. "Did you know of this, Margaux?"

"I learned of it today," Lady Margaux said quietly.

They were discussing her! Beatrice wished she could have heard the earlier part of this conversation. She stepped back further so she would not be seen and listened.

"She is here to help with the children," Rhys explained.

"That's wonderful, but I do not understand. I thought your betrothal was over. Did she choose this life instead?" Lord Ashbury sounded concerned. "That does not sound like the Lady Beatrice I know."

Yes, Rhys, please explain why I am here, Beatrice thought.

"So why is she not dining with us?" Lady Beaujolais inquired.

There was an uncomfortable silence.

"We have not seen her since this morning," Lady Mary explained.

"Should we send out a search party?" Dr. Craig sounded gravely concerned.

"She is an adult. If she has not returned by dark, I will gather everyone," Lady Mary reasoned.

"Why would she *want* to stay away?" Lady Anjou asked astutely. Her mother tried to hush her under the table.

"She is cross with me," Rhys finally admitted. "Hopefully she is merely avoiding me and is unharmed."

Should she let them know she was back? She felt like an outsider as she listened to them. She decided to let them worry. Not out of spite, but she would rather be with the children than answer tedious questions. The servants would inform Lady Mary.

The conversation quickly moved on. "Wonderful news about Bonaparte being exiled." Lord Ashbury said.

"I am thankful the tyrant has been stopped. We have lost so many men with both wars. It is time for them to return home," Dr. Craig agreed.

"Those that are left," Rhys replied sombrely.

Beatrice did not want to think about what that could mean for Nathaniel.

~

After dinner, there was a light knock on her door. Beatrice did not want to answer, but she knew she could not avoid the entire household forever. The person knocked again. "Beatrice, it is Mary. Please allow me to come in."

Beatrice especially did not wish to see her, but she did need her help to arrange a carriage to London. She rose and answered the door. She held it wide enough for Lady Mary to enter, and then gestured for her to sit down.

"Are you all right?"

Was Beatrice hearing things? Mary had not asked her that when she was kicked in the head by an angry cow. Of course, she was not all right. Her red swollen eyes were a testament to that.

"I am determined I shall be well," she managed to say civilly, "but I do think it best if I leave. If you would be so kind as to help me arrange transport for the children and myself, I would be most obliged. My father has agreed to make them his wards. If Seamus wishes to stay until school begins, I will leave that for him to decide."

Lady Mary's eyes flickered. "I wish you would stay."

Beatrice said nothing.

"I am deeply sensible of the shocking blow you have received, but Rhys did this because he cares for you." Now Beatrice knew her hearing was failing. Lady Mary was defending Rhys to her? "I see you do not believe me. I own I was not unhappy when I heard of your broken arrangement, but I have changed my mind. I feel Rhys or Dr. Craig would be fortunate to have you."

A tear trickled down Beatrice's face. No one had ever said such a kindness of her before, and it came from the most unlikely source.

"Rhys is like a son to me. He has taken care of me when he did not have to, and he lets me run the priory the way I see fit. He gives me independence which is all I have. Rhys had no hand in your reception or employment, his only wish was to save you from the horrors of the convent. He was persuaded I would look after you." Lady Mary choked with emotion and made to leave.

Beatrice reached for Mary, "You did look after me." She placed her hand on her arm. "Thank you for telling me."

Lady Mary nodded, "I will begin making arrangements tomorrow."

CHAPTER 13

The house party was a lively one, for they made a point of including the children in their activities. Lord Ashbury was fascinated with how happy the children were and how they thrived. The concept was not so outlandish that it could not be implemented in other orphanages. The main problem would be finding decent, hard-working people to run it. Lord and Lady Ashbury were occupied learning as much as possible from the Millbanks.

The remainder of the party was outside enjoying the warm sunshine. Today lawn chess was the game *du jour*. The triplets were an extremely competitive bunch. Lady Anjou and Lady Beaujolais were focused on teaching the children stratagems.

"Any day, Jolie," Anjou taunted, waiting for the next move.

"No, not the queen! Always protect the queen," Beaujolais instructed her little partner.

Lady Margaux was standing quietly by observing. Rhys knew her to be upset, and he knew he must address his blunder, but he was unsure of what would make him out to be anything other than the graceless jackanapes she must think him.

"May we talk?" Lady Margaux asked, pre-empting his speech.

"Of course." He had best think fast. He nodded and led the way down a path. He automatically started walking toward his favourite spot.

"I am sorry for waiting to tell you about Lady Beatrice. I had hoped she would be gone by now."

"I suppose I do not understand why she is here in the first place," Lady Margaux said candidly.

"Her father needed a place to send her, and I did not want her to go to a convent where she would not know anyone. The thought of her on her knees all day in prayer and silence would not have had the desired outcome. I knew that my aunt Mary would look after her here." Rhys attempted to be as honest as he could.

"I see. So she was not actually visiting sick relatives."

"Did anyone truly believe that?"

She smiled a little at that. "I suppose I am curious for the truth because it involves you and her." Lady Margaux followed Rhys's gaze across the lawn where Beatrice was playing with some children. He did not answer her immediately. The story was not his to tell, and he warred with what to divulge.

Noticing his consternation, she wrinkled her brow. "I shall forbear to press you."

"I collect you misunderstand the situation. However, I am not at liberty to disclose all of the circumstances. I am in earnest in my court of you. Had I foreseen..."

She held up her hand. "No, please. I do not question your intentions, nor do I pretend to understand what caused the rift between the two of you. Be that as it may, I want someone who looks at me the way you look at her," she said, interrupting his thoughts as she noticed him watching Beatrice longingly.

Rhys was speechless. He did not even realize he was watching Beatrice.

"I am sure you can find someone who will not countenance the fact you love someone else, but I am not the one."

"Lady Margaux, I am truly sorry." He felt like a blackguard.

She nodded, her lip trembling. "And, I know your intentions were honourable, but you still love her."

"I cannot have her," Rhys replied without emotion.

"May I still call you friend?" She managed to say with composure and gave his hand a gentle squeeze.

"You are an amazing woman, Margaux. I do not deserve your friendship, and I humbly beg your pardon." Rhys said in all earnestness.

"I can be a gracious loser." She reached up and gave him a kiss on the cheek. "Maybe it is not too late for you." Lady Margaux looked toward Beatrice then walked away.

Rhys was left standing alone, wondering how he had managed to completely make a muddle of his life. He knew Margaux was right. He was not sorry for losing her as a prospective bride, only as a friend.

Did he have to flaunt his new betrothed at every turn? Beatrice tried not to take notice of Rhys and Lady Margaux, but every time she tried to move away, they seemed to be there. She resolved to disregard them and concentrate on the children.

"You are sad since the Master arrived," Catriona observed.

"The Master and I were friends for a very long time, since I was not much older than you," Beatrice reflected.

"So why are you sad? If he is your friend, he should make you happy."

"We had a disagreement." It sounded simple when she said it aloud.

"Mama used to say we must learn to disagree without being disagreeable." Catriona dared her to contradict her mama's wisdom.

"Those are very wise words, but sometimes there are things that cannot be resolved."

Catriona shook her head. "When Seamus and I would argue, Mama would put us in a room and not let us come out until we talked about our problems."

"I will remember that next time I hear you two argue." She smiled and tweaked the girl on the nose with the touch of a finger. "Run along and play." The boys were playing rounders, and the girls were setting up a tea party with the dolls they had sewn. Catriona joined the other girls, to Beatrice's relief. She did not want to explain to a six-year-old how horribly she had behaved. She lay back on the blanket and watched the clouds. Anything to avoid seeing the happy couple.

"May I join you?" a familiar voice asked.

Beatrice looked out from the hand she had over her eyes to block the sun. "Of course, Andrew."

He sat on the blanket next to her and joined her in her cloud-watching.

"How is Elinor?" Beatrice needed to hear that she was not suffering from her horridness.

If Andrew was surprised that she asked, he hid it well. "She and Easton are revoltingly happy." He laughed. "And her child will be enormous, or there will be several."

"She is increasing?" She found she was genuinely happy for Elinor, but she found a longing in her own heart that she could not explain. "I am sure the Earl is beside himself."

Andrew nodded. "Naturally. So how are *you*, cousin?" Andrew looked her in the eye.

"I honestly do not know. If you had asked me a few days ago I would have said tolerably well."

"Then our fortuitous arrival." He laughed.

"Something of that nature." Andrew always had a way of making her laugh, no matter what the situation. He and Rhys were the two people she could be herself with. The three of them were together often after Nathaniel and Elinor had left them six years ago. Until recently, that is.

"Why did you choose to leave?" Andrew had humour, but he also had a way with words, and subtlety was not his way.

"You believe I chose this?" Beatrice was incredulous.

Andrew gave her a queer look.

"I did not *choose* this, but I cannot say I am sorry for it either."

"Dr. Craig, I presume?"

"I do not know, Andrew. I thought he was merely a friend until the morning you and Rhys walked up on us. I had given up hope of any reconciliation. Father told me Rhys was taking a bride and so, yes, I suppose I am considering his offer. However, I will be returning to London for a time. I do not wish to remain here."

"It is tiresome." They both saw the kiss that Lady Margaux planted on Vernon's cheek. He pulled a blade of grass and picked it apart. "Bea, I want you to talk with Rhys before you go. Promise?"

Beatrice glared at him. He glared back. She knew she would not win this battle from experience. "Promise," she reluctantly agreed with a sigh.

"Bea?" He held out his hand to bring her up to her feet. He grabbed her and hugged her tightly and said, "It is good to have you back."

"We have to do something, Seamus," Catriona was insistent. "They need our help. She is planning on taking all of us away to London. I heard her talking to Miss Mary about it. If we do not do something, then she might not marry Dr. Craig," she said in all of her six-year-old seriousness.

"Have you got any ideas?" Seamus asked.

Catriona shook her head.

"Might we plan a picnic and say it is for all of us and leave them alone together?" Seamus offered.

"That might work." Catriona's face lit up with excitement.

The children made plans, and then went off to ask Cook for her help.

Seamus had already completed his rounds with Dr. Craig for the day. They were not sure how they would get him to the priory without raising his suspicions. Cook was leery of a scheme to trick the good doctor, until she found out the doctor had confided to Seamus that he had offered for Beatrice. Seamus had then confided to

Catriona, who confided in Cook. *Then* Cook was more than willing to be a fellow conspirator.

"I reckon it will be all right if ye say they be betrothed," Cook reasoned.

"I think we should just invite him for a picnic," Seamus said. "Why would he be suspicious? He is here all of the time anyway."

"Perhaps yer right," Cook pondered. "Ye send over a note, 'an I'll pack up a hamper."

The children went to inform Beatrice of their intended outing. She was happy for anything that took her away from the house guests, so she was not suspicious of the impromptu picnic. They led her to the pier, which had a blanket and place settings neatly arranged with the basket of food and a bottle of wine laid out.

The children had sent a note for Dr. Craig to meet them by the pier, and he arrived not long after they did.

As soon as he said his greetings, the children remembered something they had forgotten to do for Miss Mary and promptly ran off.

"It seems our little friends are conspiring against us," Beatrice remarked. Though she was embarrassed, she was impressed with their ingenuity.

"Or *for* us," Dr. Craig said, amused. "Shall we see what they have managed to come up with?" He gestured toward the blanket and helped her sit down.

Cook had outdone herself with the basket of food. When Beatrice saw the roasted chicken she had to deter her thoughts from her little friend, the hen. She wondered if Cook had even thought about her chicken ordeal when she packed up the food. There was also fresh fruit, bread and some biscuits that were still warm from the oven.

Beatrice's stomach growled indelicately. She had not eaten much since the house party arrived.

"That reminds me. You need to eat more. Doctor's orders." He flashed her a charming smile, and then prepared a plate and handed it to her.

"I know. I have been distracted lately." She took a bite of bread, avoiding the chicken.

"It must be serious if you are forgetting to eat. This would not have anything to do with Lord Vernon?" Dr. Craig looked at her knowingly.

She nodded. She did not feel like starting off this relationship pretending. "Our fathers arranged a betrothal for us when we were children, if both parties agreed as adults. That was eleven years ago. He, Andrew and I were together much as children."

"And you are now adults," he finished the thought for her.

She nodded.

"I can see why he was vexed when he arrived and saw us. Why did you not tell me, Beatrice?"

"I never dreamt that he was the Master here and would just show up one day. We had a falling out before I left London, and I was sent away."

"And the betrothal?" he asked, and bit into a plum.

"Is over. He is betrothed to Lady Margaux now," she said matter-of-factly, though it was hard to say out loud.

"Ah. I see. Are you sure you are ready to forget him?" he asked doubtfully.

"I am not sure of anything," she replied candidly, "but I am willing to try."

"That is better than no, I suppose."

"I apologize for being vague. I am still coming to terms with the changes in my life. I plan to return to London for a while at least. I promised my father I would visit."

"Will you come back?"

"I believe so. I do not know my own heart. I think it best to see what my feelings are when I am away from here."

"I understand," he said quietly.

Beatrice hoped he did. She needed to make sure she was not making a grave mistake. Her judgement was too clouded with Rhys being near. "Let us talk of something more interesting," she said, wanting to lighten the mood. She thought for a moment. "Where did you grow up?"

"I am not sure that qualifies as more interesting."

"I do not know much about you," she countered.

"Verra well, but I warned you." He laughed. "I spent my childhood in a small village on Loch Lomond. I went to school in Edinburgh. After that I went into the army, and now I am here."

She gave him her best impression of exasperated. "Please omit the details."

"I answered the question," he parried.

Beatrice reflected as she conversed with him, that one could not deny his address, easy manners and devastating smile. He was handsome and intelligent, and she enjoyed being around him, which were all encouraging discoveries to her. She had never pondered any one other than Rhys, so she had not considered what it would mean to marry another.

"Do you have any family? You mentioned being a second son, once."

"Aye, I have an older brother who still lives on the loch at the family estate." He raised his eyebrows to see if he could get away with stopping there.

"And?" She waved her hand in the air encouragingly.

"He enjoys the arts of distilling whisky and producing children."

"I will not force information from you." She said the words playfully, but stood up and brushed her skirts out.

"There is not much to me, but I am quite content. I live in a beautiful place; I am able to help people every day, and I am surrounded by good people. That is enough for me."

The last point was intriguing to her, and she pondered it as she walked toward the end of the pier. What would it be like to be wholly content with who you were and where you were, and what you were doing with your life? Could she be content as a doctor's wife in remote Scotland? She sat ungracefully on the pier and dangled her legs off the end like she had as a child.

Gavin eventually followed and joined her on the pier. There was a mirror image of the mountain reflected in the perfectly still water, except for the occasional fish breaking the surface. She felt an inner peace she did not know she had been missing. She was comfortable with him, even if her heart did not flutter when she was with him. Gavin took her hand in his and slowly rubbed hers with his thumb, and she leaned her head over on to his shoulder. They stayed there in silent tranquillity until they heard the priory bells ringing, signalling tea-time.

CHAPTER 14

*B*eatrice did not want to leave the comfort of her bed this morning. The weather had turned cool, and the skies were dark, signalling imminent rain. She decided to forgo her morning walk and remain in her bed a little longer. She snuggled her coverlet tighter at the chilly breeze coming in her window. Lady Mary had finally arranged for her and the children to leave two days hence.

She heard an equipage pull into the drive in front of the house. Who could be visiting so early? It would not be Dr. Craig, for he would park his gig at the stable. Struggling with curiosity, she debated climbing out from under her warm covers, when she heard voices. She lay still so she could hear.

"While I am sorry you and Margaux did not find you would suit, I am most pleased with your orphanage and feel that some benefit will come from the visit," Lord Ashbury's voice boomed in the vacant courtyard.

Curiosity won. Beatrice hopped out of bed and ran over to look out of the window. Rhys and Lord Ashbury were shaking hands. Could it be true? Lord Ashbury went back into the house, and Andrew and Rhys were still talking.

"Must you leave too?" Rhys asked Andrew.

"I must rejoin Wellington. You are on your own with this. I cannot help you with Bea, but I insist you talk to her."

"She does not want to talk to me," Rhys said and kicked some stones on the drive with his boot, and they began walking the other direction from Beatrice's room.

They walked out of her earshot. Who could he need to talk to? Lady Margaux? A small rush of excitement went through her. If he and Lady Margaux did not suit, then did she still have a chance? Would he even consider renewing his suit if he believed her reformed?

She should not cherish false hope. She was leaving in two days. That had already been arranged. At the very least, she would try to talk to him today like she promised Andrew. She needed to make amends, if nothing else.

Rhys saw Andrew and the Ashbury family off. What a disaster. He did not deserve the kindness they showed him. Aunt Mary had also informed him that Beatrice and the Douglas children would be leaving in a couple of days. Perhaps that would be for the best. Beatrice had avoided him at every turn. What was he to do now? Would this never end? He decided a long hard ride was in order. He looked at the ominous clouds overhead and decided a ride in the rain was fitting.

He gathered his riding gear and marched toward the stables. He chose his favourite gelding, The Bruce, and set off, hoping to clear his mind and make a new plan.

Rhys and The Bruce followed the river taking the path that went around the loch, where the peace and serenity were just the calm he needed to think. He stopped for a while to let The Bruce rest and have a drink. His mind was clear, but he still could not come up with any solutions other than to give up on marriage and allow his brother to inherit. He struggled with his emotions. It was not that his brother was not good enough; he was a right one. It must be the male sense of wanting to spread his seed, he reasoned.

Rhys had always thought he would have a house full of hazel-eyed, auburn-haired brats running around. He had looked forward to teaching his sons to hunt and fish and to dancing at balls with his little girls. He skimmed rocks across the water in frustration. He could not fully come to terms with giving up.

He would have to find someone else and try again.

Rhys mounted the horse and rode off again. They rode up the mountain as the rain started to fall. The rain beating in his face was almost cathartic. The Bruce was not in agreement and began to grow skittish as thunder and lightning grew closer and the storm became fiercer.

A loud pop of thunder caused the horse to rear, forelegs striking at the sky. Rhys slipped in his seat, but managed to hold on. The normally steady horse was not going to take much more. Rhys's voice sang a calming chant to soothe the nervous horse. He turned The Bruce around and began heading back down the mountain to look for shelter until the storm passed.

Rhys could feel his control rapidly deteriorating as they continued down the steep path. The horse was frightened and wanted to gallop. Rhys decided to dismount and try leading the horse. Just as he began to slide from the saddle, another loud crack of thunder exploded, and Rhys was thrown from the gelding when he reared.

Beatrice watched as Rhys headed toward the stables and rode off. Bother! Why had not she learned to ride better? She had been taught to ride, but she was terrified of horses and had avoided riding from fear. She did not think she would be able to catch him, even if she knew where he was going and could muster up the courage. She would have to delay speaking to him.

Beatrice struggled to concentrate on her tasks as she waited. She kept watching out of the window for Rhys to return. The children were as restless as she felt being stuck inside during the rain. It began to grow stormy, and she became sick with apprehension. Where could he be? Pray, he was able to find shelter. He was an experienced rider, so she knew she was fretting for no reason, but she could not help herself.

Tea-time came and went. Dinner was served to the children, but Beatrice waited for Rhys to return so she could talk to him then. She finally sought out Lady Mary to voice her concerns when he had not arrived by dinner. Perhaps he had told his aunt where he was going.

Beatrice knocked on the parlour door.

"Enter." Beatrice came into the room. Mary looked up from her mending and saw her face and was immediately concerned. "Whatever is the matter?"

"Have you seen Rhys? He went riding this morning and has not returned. Please tell me he was going somewhere so I can cease my anxieties."

Lady Mary shook her head. "I am unaware of any plans."

One of the grooms knocked on the open door.

"Yes, Tommy?" Lady Mary asked worriedly.

"The Master's horse has returned without him," Tommy said solemnly.

"No! No!" Beatrice began to weep, assuming the worst.

Lady Mary shook Beatrice. "This is not the time for histrionics. We need you to think before we send anyone out this late with the tracks muddied."

Beatrice tried to dry up her tears so she could help.

"You were apparently the last one who saw him. Did you see which way he went?"

Beatrice nodded. "He rode along the river path toward the loch."

Tommy agreed, "That is 'is favourite ride. We can start there. I just hope 'e dinna head up the mountain in that storm."

Beatrice rose to go help with the search.

"Where are you going?"

"To help look for Rhys." Where else would she go?

"Nonsense. It is dark, and you do not know your way. I have not seen you on a horse the entire time you have been at the priory."

"But I found Seamus!" Beatrice argued.

"That was during the day, Beatrice," Lady Mary reasoned. "Do not be alarmed. They will find him."

"I am going at first light if he's not yet back," Beatrice replied stubbornly, but she knew Lady Mary was right.

Beatrice tucked the children into bed and read them a story to help pass the time. She decided after waiting for two hours that it was the worst form of torture. She would rather scrub floors all day than wait, unable to do anything. Mary tried to talk her into going to bed, but the thought of sleep at this point was preposterous. She tried to embroider, but threw the tambour frame down after a few poor stitches.

Lady Mary retired to her room, but Beatrice refused to lie in a comfortable bed when Rhys was out there somewhere in the cold. Thank God it was summer; she refused to think of how horrible the outcome might be in winter. Her mind drifted to all the worst possible course of events, and she cried until she dozed.

She awoke to the sounds of horses and ran to the door to see if Rhys was there. Several of the men looked haggard and exhausted, but she did not see Rhys among them.

Noticing the worried look on her face, one of the men said, "'E weren't on the loch path, Miss. 'E must have gone up the mountain. We came back fer fresh horses an' a quick meal."

Beatrice nodded. Why had she not thought about food? She could have spent her energies productively. "I will go and tell Cook to prepare something."

The men left to wash and rub down the horses. Beatrice went to the kitchen to see if she could help. She needed to be busy. Cook had already anticipated feeding the men, and was frying bacon and pulling fresh scones from the oven.

The men filed in, and Beatrice helped to serve them. They were disturbingly quiet as they ate. Bea was hoping to hear something encouraging, but the only thing she learned was that Dr. Craig had joined the search. He had apparently seen evidence of a landslide on the side of the mountain and went to start looking there.

Beatrice did not think her heart could hurt any more than it already did, but she was wrong.

~

Beatrice tried to help clear up after breakfast, but the other servants told her they would manage. She headed out toward the river path. She knew she could not do much, but she could not sit idly any longer.

Beatrice was not sure where the mountain path started. She could see where the landslide happened from across the loch, and headed in that direction. She was exhausted when she finally found the track. She cursed her fear of animals. She could have been here ages ago if she was not such a coward.

She was struggling to climb the mountain path. She knew the men had come this way because of the evidence from the horses, but would she ever find them? A few times she thought she heard voices but then she could not find anyone. When she finally made it to the area where she thought the slide to be, she saw one of the men. She did not know his name, but she recognized his face.

"Is there any news of the Master?" she asked anxiously.

"Aye, lass. He fell in a gorge. The doctor and Tommy scaled down te retrieve 'im."

Retrieve him? "Is he, is he..." She could not bring herself to say the word.

The man shook his head. "The doctor says 'es still alive, but hurt verra bad. 'E says is head is hurt an' 'is leg is broke."

Beatrice nodded and began running until she found the search party. They were hoisting Rhys up with ropes. When they reached the top, Dr. Craig pulled himself over the edge first to make sure Rhys was not injured further by their efforts.

Beatrice stood back and watched, shaking with fear.

When they had him on the ground, it was all she could do not to run to him. Rhys was covered in blood and mud. Dr. Craig placed himself up on his horse and then directed the men to lift Rhys on the horse in front of him so he could support him. He had somehow managed to fashion a makeshift splint for Rhys's leg while in the gorge.

The other men mounted their horses and began the caravan down the mountain. When Tommy spotted her, he immediately jumped off his horse and offered it to her. She shook her head. "Absolutely not. I can walk. You have been working tirelessly all night. It would not be right."

Tommy's eyes grew wide and he looked acutely uncomfortable. He did not know how to respond, but he knew he could not let a lady walk.

Dr. Craig looked over and said, "Ride with her."

Tommy looked to Beatrice, who nodded. She was not as afraid if someone else was controlling the horse, and that way Tommy would not have to walk. He helped her up then mounted behind her. She was grateful for the ride. Her feet were exhausted, and she was thankful they had found Rhys alive.

Despite being on horses, it felt like an eternity before they reached the house. They had to move slowly to not injure Rhys further. The men carried Rhys to his bedroom, and Dr. Craig began to work cleaning him.

Beatrice waited in the hall until Dr. Craig was finished examining Rhys. She had sent for hot bricks and warm water in case they needed to warm him, like they had Seamus. She had no idea what supplies to ask for, so she asked one of the servants to retrieve Seamus. He had been helping Dr. Craig for several months and was more knowledgeable than anyone, save the doctor.

Seamus arrived and timidly gave Beatrice a hug. Then he went in the room to see how he could help. Beatrice passed the time pacing the hallway, nearly wearing a hole in the carpet.

CHAPTER 15

*D*r. Craig opened the door and motioned for Beatrice to enter. She looked toward Rhys lying on the bed and then back to the doctor. He nodded, and she walked toward the bed. She could not stop the cry that escaped her. Rhys was almost unrecognisable. His face was swollen and bruised, and a large gash covered the side of his head.

She reached out to hold his hand that had slipped out from under the blankets. It was covered in scratches. She pulled it to her cheek.

"He's freezing."

Dr. Craig nodded. "He was wet and in the cold all night. I have sent Seamus for supplies so I can repair his head and leg."

Beatrice had forgotten about the leg. He was covered in several thick layers to warm him.

"How bad is his leg?"

"I will need to reset it when Seamus returns with the laudanum."

She nodded. That sounded horrid.

"How long will he sleep?"

Dr. Craig hesitated. "There is a chance he willna wake up from the coma."

"What is a coma? And don't wrap it in clean linen, please!" She

139

looked up for answers. She was trying to understand. She did not want her delicate sensibilities to prevent a full accounting. If Rhys was going to die, she needed to know.

"It is similar to sleep, but the person cannot wake up. It happens with a blow to the head. It can last a few hours or a few days. The danger grows the longer it lasts, because a person canna go indefinitely without food and water."

"Is there no way to feed him?" Beatrice was trying not to panic.

Dr. Craig shrugged. "I doona know. In school, they talked about the Ancient Egyptians making a tube from reeds and animal bladders that goes to the stomach. I heard a doctor tried a few years ago with whale bone and eel skin. They pour liquid food through it."

Beatrice made a face.

"Maybe it will not come to that, it is still too early to speculate. He is breathing, and his posture is normal. His pupils are slow but still reacting."

Dr. Craig might as well have been speaking Greek, but he made it sound as if those things were positive. She understood the part about him breathing.

"Have you seen anything of this nature before?"

"Once in the army, but those injuries were more severe. It is difficult to say with a knock to the head. His body may have shut down as a preservation tactic or from shock. He might wake when he is warmed, as Seamus did."

Beatrice was confused and overwhelmed. She needed assurance that he would recover. Dr. Craig reached out and gave her hand a reassuring touch. He brought a chair over next to the bed so she could sit with Rhys.

"Thank you, Gavin."

"I am going to wash. I will be back when Seamus returns."

Beatrice nodded and sat down. She put Rhys's hand between hers and held it against her head, willing him to live. "Do not dare die on me, Rhys. Do not dare."

She heard the door close behind her.

~

As Beatrice sat with him, Rhys slowly began to warm up, but had shown no signs of waking.

Dr. Craig returned a few minutes later and began to set tools out on a table. What was he going to do to him? Beatrice watched in amazement. She longed for a fraction of Elinor's knowledge at that moment. She wanted desperately to help Rhys.

Dr. Craig was ready to begin. "If you want to wait downstairs, I will find you as soon as I finish."

Beatrice shook her head vehemently. She would not leave him. If Elinor could stand it, so could she.

He gave her a sceptical look, "Verra well, but it will not be easy."

"I understand."

Thus began the arduous task of cleaning, resetting the leg and suturing the wounds. Seamus assisted him with the tasks, remaining calm and knowing what tools were needed. Rhys grimaced and groaned in pain, which Dr. Craig thought a good sign. Beatrice had to look away most of the time and was close to being sick several times. She felt herself swaying and cold perspiration on her forehead, but she was determined to support Rhys through this ordeal. How did doctors do such monstrous things? She'd had no notion what they did other than prescribe tinctures or salves before today.

Dr. Craig finished and washed his hands in the basin. He came over to where Beatrice stood, looking exhausted, "I have done all I can for now. There is a good chance he will wake when the laudanum wears off. His leg is in poor condition. I hope I saved it, but there is a high risk of infection." He gathered his bags to leave. "I am going to rest and see my other patients. I will be back later."

"Thank you," Beatrice said quietly.

He nodded. "Lass, you need to understand he may not be the same if he awakens." He turned and left quietly with Seamus.

What could he mean? Beatrice walked back over to the bed and stroked Rhys's rogue hair back off his brow. She felt so helpless. She was filled with despair as tears began streaming down her face. She covered her mouth to quieten the sobs that threatened. She felt a pair of arms come around her. She had not realized anyone was in the room. Lady Mary pulled her close and stroked her back as they cried together.

"You need to rest, Beatrice. I can stay with him for now. It will do him no good if you exhaust yourself."

"I am not leaving him. I want him to know I am here. I want to be who he sees when he opens his eyes."

"If I cannot convince you to go to your room, I will have a cot set up in here. You will have to sleep sometime." Beatrice nodded. "I am going to send word to his mother. She needs to know."

Lady Mary left quietly. Beatrice needed to write a letter too. A long overdue letter.

⟨~⟩

Elinor,

Forgive my conveyance of this through a letter. I fervently beg for your forgiveness, though it is undeserved. I have committed the grossest of offences against you, and do not know if I will ever be able to make them up to you. I am grateful for my time away, for I have learned to understand how wronged you were, and how despicable my actions were. I had only been viewing the world through the narrowest of lenses and was unable to look beyond to see anyone save myself. I hope one day you may find it in your heart to forgive me.

I regretfully bear the news, but Rhys was hurt in a riding accident yesterday when his horse bolted during a storm. At this time, his outcome is yet unknown. He suffered a blow to the head and a broken leg. He has yet to awaken. I am most envious of your medical abilities and wish I had more to offer Rhys, but Dr. Craig is most capable and attentive. It was he who found Rhys and rescued him. I still cannot help but wish I were as knowledgeable as you. Please write with any guidance.

Congratulations on your forthcoming addition. I am sincerely happy for you.

Yours, etc.

Beatrice

~

Days. *Days* later, Rhys still remained in this coma-like state. She had lost count of how many. Beatrice felt numb. She was trying to remain hopeful, as Dr. Craig was, but it was a struggle for Rhys to swallow enough liquid, and they had not yet tried food. The doctor was contemplating how to fashion a tube to feed him, for small sips of beef broth could not sustain him indefinitely.

Dr. Craig had no explanation for why he would not awaken. His wounds were healing nicely, if any wound could be called *nice*. His muscles were beginning to wither from lying in bed, though Gavin tediously massaged his arms and legs, avoiding the break, and moved them methodically for exercise. He claimed that helped the muscles from getting so weak.

Beatrice could not understand why he could not wake up. He looked like he should open his eyes and start talking to her at any moment.

She had finally reached the point where she had to leave the room for fresh air. She never left for long because she wanted to be there when he opened his eyes for the first time. She had taken some short walks and had even visited the old priory chapel from time to time. She had never been very religious, but some of the old messages had endured. *Lean on him in times of trial. Cast your burdens upon him. God will not give you more than you can bear.*

What did they mean precisely? How did one believe in something you could not see? She wanted to believe in God. She thought she did, but she did not understand why bad things were happening. Rhys did not deserve this. She deserved to be in his place! Surely God would not punish her by letting this happen to Rhys? She did not make a habit of talking to God, and she did not know if he would hear her, but she was willing to try anything.

God, please put me in his place. He does not deserve this! I will do anything you ask of me if you will bring him back. Please God, please.

Beatrice was pretty certain she should not bargain with God either. She stood to leave when she realized she had been gone too long, and made her way back to Rhys's room. She passed Catriona on the way and felt guilty about abandoning the children. Catriona wanted to know how the Master was.

Beatrice asked, "Would you like to see him?" Catriona nodded, and Beatrice took her hand and led her into his room.

Catriona walked quietly up to his bed and looked carefully at Rhys. "Is he sleeping?"

"It is similar to that. He cannot seem to wake up."

"My mama and papa looked like they were sleeping," Catriona said, still pondering the Master.

"Yes, but the Master is still alive, Catriona," Beatrice reminded Catriona—and herself.

"Does he not want to wake up?" she asked innocently.

Beatrice pondered the question. Surely Rhys wanted to wake up? She was being absurd. "Of course he wishes to wake up."

"Maybe he can hear you. You should talk to him and say you're sorry for your disagreement."

"Perhaps I should do that." Beatrice pondered the futility of speaking to someone in a coma.

"Mama always said the angels were listening. So if the Master is still alive, why could not he hear you?"

Why indeed?

Beatrice gave her a hug and a kiss on the cheek and Catriona went back to her lessons.

Beatrice looked back at Rhys lying on the bed. *Was it possible he could hear her?* She studied his familiar form from across the room, watching his chest rise and fall. *Why will he not wake up?*

She sat next to him and took his hand in hers. "Rhys? Rhys, can you hear me? It's Bea." She felt a little ridiculous and was unsure of what to say, so she poured her heart out. "I need you to wake up. I cannot bear to lose you." She paused to try to compose herself. She put her head down and continued while stroking his hand gently. "I have so many things to say to you, but mostly I am sorry. I do not know what happened those last few months, but they were the loneliest months of my life. I could feel you slipping away from me, and I did not know how to stop it. I beg your forgiveness. Please wake up and tell me this was a horrible nightmare, and we can go back to the way things were."

She looked up to wipe her tears and saw Rhys's eyes were open.

CHAPTER 16

*R*hys?" Beatrice's heart was going to leap from her chest. She jumped up so he could see her, but he was staring blankly at the ceiling. "Rhys," she said his name again, but his eyes did not move. "Can you hear me? Squeeze my hand if you can hear me."

He closed his eyes again.

"No! Do not leave me!" she shouted and shook his arm, but there was no response. She sat back down and stared at him.

Lady Mary came into the room. "Is something the matter?"

"Yes. No. I do not know! He opened his eyes for a moment but closed them again," Beatrice said, disheartened.

"I think that is a good sign, but we should send for the doctor."

Beatrice nodded. She needed to know what that meant.

It was not long before Dr. Craig returned. He felt it was a very good sign that Rhys had opened his eyes. "I have been reading what little I have available about this in my journals. The theory is, when the swelling goes down inside his head, he can begin to wake up. Not verra much else is known, but if he has opened his eyes, he may be starting to improve. In one case, I read the patient's wakefulness lasted a short time at first, and then began lasting longer. In another, the patient woke up and immediately started talking."

Either way, Beatrice thought there was a reason to hope. There was no more eye-opening that day, but the next morning Beatrice began talking to him again, and his eyes opened. It did last longer, and Rhys blinked once. Beatrice began to cry in happiness, and she saw one tear fall from his eye. For the first time since his accident, she started to believe he was still alive inside.

Later that day when Dr. Craig was exercising Rhys's muscles, he opened his eyes again. He looked at the doctor, then observed what he was doing to his legs.

Beatrice noticed his confusion and took his hand in hers. "Rhys, this is Dr. Craig. He is trying to help you. You had an accident and have been asleep for several days." Rhys turned his head and looked at her, devoid of emotion. He made eye contact with her, then turned his head back the other way.

"Please leave."

She stood there stunned. *Did he say to leave?*

Without turning his head to look at her, he said quietly, "Please leave me, Bea. Do not make this harder than it must be."

She could not seem to move. She could not be hearing him properly. All she could manage was shaking her head in denial as her throat swelled and tightened to fight back tears.

Dr. Craig came over to her side and with a gentle pressure on her back, guided her toward the door. "Just give him some time, lass," Gavin spoke quietly to her. "He just woke up. I am sure he will feel like talking to you later."

She looked away to hide the tears and went out of the door. This was not what she had imagined when he finally awoke.

Dr. Craig walked back over to Rhys's bedside. "You canna feel your leg, can you?"

Rhys was still looking at the wall, but he shook his head.

"May I examine you more? It will help me to ken where you do have feeling."

Rhys shrugged his shoulders.

The doctor touched his leg in several places, pushed on him and moved the limb in different directions as best he could. "There is still a chance it will recover feeling. You have good circulation to the leg, and it has only been a few days. It is early to say for sure. I am going to write to a colleague in Edinburgh who specializes in orthopaedics to see if he has experience of this."

Rhys did not respond, he just kept staring at the wall.

"I will come back later when you have had some time to think."

The doctor packed his bag and Vernon said, "She needs to leave."

Dr. Craig did not turn around but said, "The lass has not left your side the entire time. She has been worrying herself sick about you." He shook his head in disbelief and left.

Beatrice shut the door behind her and walked down the hall. It hurt to breathe, and it felt like the walls were closing in on her. She kept walking, in a daze, and with no thought in her mind other than to get away before giving way to her grief. She needed to be alone. She walked out of the door, and her feet seemed to take her to the priory's chapel.

She was not sure why she kept being led to this old chapel. Perhaps it was a place to find solitude, or perhaps there was a deeper meaning. Either way she found herself sitting in the pew staring up at the stained-glass window. She laughed in a mocking way to herself. She looked up at the glass and towards the heavens and said, "I suppose you did answer my prayer. I did not understand I needed to be more specific."

Beatrice was grateful that Rhys had awoken, but she could not stop thinking about what he had said to her. She supposed she deserved this, but she had hoped they could at least be friends again one day. She decided to take a chance and say another prayer.

God, please let Rhys find it in his heart to forgive me. Please give me the strength to be the friend he needs.

She sat there a while longer trying to assimilate what had happened, when Gavin took the seat next to her.

"Are you all right?" He put his arm around her shoulder and kissed the top of her head.

Beatrice began to nod and then she shook her head. "I am not sure. It was rather unexpected, but deserved."

"No, lass. I wanted you to understand. Lord Vernon canna feel one of his legs," Gavin said softly.

Beatrice let out a gasp and covered her mouth.

"I think he does not want you to see him like that. It is frightening to think you might not be able to walk again. He thinks it better for you if he pushes you away."

"*Will* he be able to walk again?" Beatrice asked, afraid of the answer. Gavin reached out and wiped away the tear that was trickling down her face.

"I doona know. It is too soon to be certain. I am going to Edinburgh to search the medical library and to see a consulting physician and see if he has any suggestions."

"What can I do? I feel helpless. He does not want to see me," she said hopelessly.

"You need to use your instinct. He has been your best friend for eleven years," he said calmly.

She shook her head. "I do not trust my instincts."

"I think he is hurting inside as well as outside, and sometimes you have to heal one to heal the other. He will need his friends verra badly to see him through this."

"What would you do, Gavin?" She looked up into his cerulean eyes searching for wisdom.

"I wouldna' turn my back on my friend, no matter what he said." He kissed her on the head again and stood to leave.

"Gavin?" He looked down at her so tenderly her heart ached. She did not believe she deserved him either. "Thank you."

∼

Beatrice grudgingly made her way back to the house. She knew she could not turn her back on Rhys and just leave, but she also did not know how she was going to help him. She had known him for eleven years, but she had no experience with this stubborn side of him. Until her last day at Loring Abbey, they had never spoken a cross word to one another.

Beatrice tried to think of something, but Rhys was always the pacifier, never the offender. She tried to think of some experience that might help her, but the only example she could recollect was her father, and her mother's hysterics in response. No, that was not helpful in the least.

Beatrice walked through the door and heard the voice to squash any last hope of reconciling with Rhys. His mother, the Countess—her mother's enemy and her adversary. Beatrice did not personally dislike his mother, but the Countess had transferred her hate for Beatrice's mother to her. Beatrice did not know whether to listen, to greet her, or to keep on going. Once again she found herself overhearing conversations. A year ago, she would have enjoyed listening for any gossip to share with her mother. But now she did not want any confrontation, fearing it would only harm Rhys.

The Countess was already berating her. "I am sorry, Mary, but people do not change their colours. Give her a week back in London, and she will go back to the way she was."

"I remember your letters about her, Louise. I, too, was prejudiced against her when she arrived. But I am telling you this is not the same person. She has worked hard and not complained about anything we have asked her to do. She has taken a gentleman's orphaned children under her wing and loved them like her own. She has not left my nephew's side since he was injured. So, no, I will not ask her to leave."

"Very well. I will judge for myself, but if I think she is hurting my son, I will personally escort her off the estate."

Beatrice did not want to hear any more. She walked into the room in all civility and made a curtsy to the Countess. "Lady Vernon, I am glad you are here. For Rhys's sake, can we agree to be pleasant?"

The Countess was clearly shocked by Beatrice's forwardness, but when she saw the sincerity of her statement, she nodded. "Very well, Lady Beatrice, but only for my son."

The Countess immediately excused herself to rest after her journey.

Beatrice turned to Lady Mary and said, "She thinks me a heartless shrew like my mother."

Lady Mary said, "This may be the time to act the heartless shrew."

"Whatever can you mean?" Beatrice was confused.

"I mean you will have to forget your heart while dealing with my nephew for the foreseeable future. He is not himself at present, and you will have to ignore what he says to you. It will hurt your heart. He does not mean the things he is saying. You know him as well as anyone, and I truly believe you are the only one who can save him from himself."

"So I am to ignore his wishes and march right into his room?" she asked in disbelief.

"If necessary, then yes, that is what I am saying," Lady Mary said candidly.

"I do not know what to do with him."

"Make him smile again. That is a good place to start."

CHAPTER 17

*B*eatrice hesitated but nodded and went to Rhys's room. She held her hand up to knock, but then thought better of it. He would not welcome her. She slowly let herself into the room. Rhys's eyes were open, but he was staring out of the window. She acknowledged his valet with a nod of her head, and the man crept out of the room.

Beatrice walked over and sat in her usual chair next to the bed, and waited for Rhys to tell her to leave. She was nervous. She had no idea what she would say to him.

He remained mute. She was beginning to think that was worse. She had sat in this room in complete quiet for days, but nothing quite compared to being deliberately ignored. She endured the silent treatment until it was time for his medicine and exercise. She did not know when the doctor was to return, and he was relying on them to continue his therapeutic regimen.

She prepared his medicines in a cordial and held it up to his lips to drink. Rhys stared at the cup, clearly debating whether or not to comply.

"You must co-operate or I will force the medicine into you." His eyes widened in surprise. "I have learned much from dealing with the children these last months."

"Why?" Rhys whispered.

"Because we need to perform your exercises, and Dr. Craig says the medicine helps the pain."

"Will you not let me suffer in peace? Must you shame me thus?" He raised his voice to emphasize his point.

"Oh." *That's why.* "I prefer to look on it as helping an old friend."

"Dear God. Your pretty doctor has convinced you to be his nurse! You think that will make you happy in a few years, Bea?"

"That is unfair. *My* pretty doctor has gone to Edinburgh to try to help you. Now open up." She would ignore the remainder of that question. She was unsure of her answer.

Surprisingly, he complied. She moved to the foot of the bed to begin his exercises. She had seen Gavin do these for days, and it looked so simple when he did them, though she had not actually *looked* at the leg. She had never touched a man's leg before and hesitated before pulling the cover back. Perhaps she should ask the valet to assist her. She must have contorted her face in confusion, for Rhys commented, "Are you not relieved? You do not have to be stuck with a cripple now."

"Relieved would not be my word of choice, Rhys." She went to ring for the valet. "The look on my face was from noticing the anatomical differences in your legs and mine." She tried not to blush. Who knew a man's feet were so big and their legs so hairy? The valet knocked and entered the room.

"Samuels, do you think you might be able to assist with the exercises Dr. Craig was performing? He had to leave for Edinburgh, so it is left to us." She was still blushing. Samuels nodded. She looked away from the leg while Samuels moved it back and forth.

"The doctor mentioned having him sit in a chair for a few minutes, if he is agreeable, afterwards."

Samuels nodded to her. "Yes, my lady."

Beatrice and Samuels helped him into the chair after the exercises were finished. Rhys looked exhausted. "Bea, why are you here?"

"Did you hear any of what I said to you when you were sleeping?" His expression softened. Maybe he had heard. "I am not leaving until you are better. Or at least well enough to throw me out yourself." She smiled the first genuine smile she had felt in ages.

Rhys could not help but crack a little smile back. "That could be some time."

Exactly. She was rather pleased how easily her first goal was accomplished.

There was a commotion in the courtyard. Who could be here now? It had only been two days since Gavin left for Edinburgh. She supposed it could be him. Beatrice looked out of the window into the drive, and there was not one, not two, but *three* carriages. What was happening? She saw crests on all three conveyances but was too far away to recognize them. She did, however, recognize Lord Easton as he alighted from the equipage. Easton held out his hand and a very rotund Elinor gingerly climbed out with two men helping her and fussing over her.

What were they thinking to come all of this way with her in a delicate condition? Beatrice felt a rush of relief and gratitude wash over her. The help would be most welcome with Rhys. If surrounded by his friends and family, it could only help. He would not be allowed to feel sorry for himself with them present. Beatrice thought that if Elinor had come so far, she must have received her letter and left almost as soon as it had arrived. Hopefully, that meant she might be able to forgive her one day. But, if she only came to help Rhys, that was enough to satisfy her for now.

Beatrice rushed down to the courtyard to greet her family.

"I cannot believe you are here!" Beatrice exclaimed as she rushed over to greet the arrivals.

"How is he?" Lord Easton asked, concerned.

"He is awake now, but has no feeling in one of his legs. Dr. Craig has gone to Edinburgh to consult the medical libraries and specialists in the field."

Elinor nodded. Beatrice looked to her, uncertain of the response she would get. "Welcome, cousin. I cannot believe you came so far in your condition!"

"Against my recommendations. I could not keep her away," Easton said, exasperated.

"But with Dr. McGinnis's permission. Your Dr. Craig is more than capable of caring for me if needed. I can have babies anywhere," Elinor stated as if they were making a fuss over nothing.

"Thank you for coming." Beatrice's eyes filled with tears, and Elinor attempted to hug her as best she could with her expanded stomach.

"I trust I can help," Elinor said hopefully.

"Merely being here helps," Beatrice said gratefully.

The door to the next carriage opened and the men went over to assist the passenger out. The Earl had apparently suffered the journey as well with Sir Charles. Beatrice watched in amazement as they climbed from the carriage. She looked at the third carriage and wondered if her other cousin, Sarah, would be joining them too.

Beatrice walked over to greet her uncle and the Earl. Seeing the look on her face, Sir Charles chuckled. "Did you think we were going to miss out? Of course we care about Vernon, but I am not about to miss the birth of my grandchild. I missed the last one."

The third carriage opened, and Adam and Susie jumped out and ran to their new mama and papa, much to their nursemaid's chagrin. The children were introduced to Beatrice, and their presence was explained, though she was not surprised that Easton and Elly had fallen in love with the children. She felt the same way about the Douglas children.

"Let us go inside. The children will be delighted to have new friends to play with, and I am sure Lady Mary and Lady Vernon will be thrilled to see you all."

Beatrice led them to the morning room, where she expected Lady Mary and the Countess to be, but Elinor and Easton begged to be shown to Vernon first.

"Go on ahead, Bea," her uncle Charles reassured her. "We can see to ourselves."

~

Beatrice led them up to Rhys's room. She lightly tapped on the door and leaned her head in. "Rhys? You have some visitors."

"I am not fit to see anyone, Bea," Rhys replied grumpily.

Easton pushed the door in and said, "We are not anyone. Do not forget I have seen you much worse than this."

Elinor followed him into the room. Rhys looked at her in shock.

"I am merely with child. You are not actually seeing an elephant," Elly said light-heartedly.

He was too stunned for humour. He had never seen a woman so large with child before. "I am merely astonished to see you here. Are you sure it's safe?"

"Do not encourage her, Vernon," Easton warned.

Elinor walked over to him and took his hand. "I am so happy to see you awake. We were not sure how we would find you."

"Yes, I am awake. I survived Salamanca, and I get taken down by a thunderstorm," he said dryly.

"You will not be down for long if we have anything to say about it," Elinor pronounced.

Rhys smiled, then looked away. "Unless you can perform a miracle, I am bound for a Bath chair with your father, Easton. The Earls are starting a new fashion," he said sarcastically.

Elinor could abide this talk no more. "May I look at your leg? I know I am not Dr. Craig, but I am fascinated nonetheless."

Rhys waved his hand for her to help herself. "You can do no harm as it is."

Elinor pulled back the covers from his leg. There was still a splint in place over the area where the leg was broken. "I am going to touch your leg in a few places, so close your eyes and tell me when you can feel my touch."

Beatrice interrupted her, "May I retrieve Seamus?"

Elinor nodded and looked at Rhys curiously while Beatrice ran out of the room.

Rhys explained that Seamus had been an apprentice to Dr. Craig, and they were sending him to school in the autumn.

"Dr. McGinnis is offering similar studies at our new school. We are not training doctors, however. Most of the students will become surgeons or apothecaries, but I am enjoying learning everything I can from him myself."

Seamus returned, introductions were made, and Elly proceeded with her examination. "Please close your eyes."

"Why does he have to do that?" Seamus questioned.

"It helps me to know what he feels versus what he sees," Elinor explained.

She then pushed with her fingers in a few places and had Seamus feel in the same place. "Those are his pulses." Seamus had already been taught about those.

"Yes. So it is unusual that his pulses are strong, yet he has no feeling. I see why Dr. Craig went to see a consulting specialist. The only thing I can think of is that perhaps something dislodged when the bone was reset. But I am no surgeon."

Seamus explained that Dr. Craig had been doing exercises to keep Rhys's leg strong.

"That is exactly what Dr. McGinnis would have done. I am afraid I do not have anything to add. I agree that Dr. Craig is right to consult the speciality doctors. I might suggest you remove from the bed. It is not healthy to lie in bed all day. For broken bones, or for very pregnant ladies." She shot Easton a look as if he had been trying to make her do just that.

"Perhaps we can steal Father's chair and take you out for some fresh air today," Easton offered.

"I think that an excellent idea." Rhys seemed enthusiastic for the first time since he had awoken.

A day later, Dr. Craig returned from Edinburgh with Dr. Murray, a surgeon who specialized in orthopaedics. After going through the process of examining Vernon in extreme detail, the surgeon determined that an operation would be necessary in order to release the nerve that was being compressed.

Dr. Craig explained. Dr. Charles Bell, whom they studied medicine with and later worked with in the army, had recently discovered that nerves had different functions as they left the spinal cord. Some nerves provided sensory function and some provided function for movement. "I first thought to contact Dr. Murray because of my exposure to Dr. Bell's work. I ken it was most likely a damaged nerve for the circulation remained intact."

Dr. Craig demonstrated this by having Lord Vernon move his toes which shocked everyone. "This demonstrates that the damage is in the leg, not from the spinal cord in his back, where the nerves come back together in the spine and send the messages to the brain."

"Fascinating," Elinor exclaimed.

Rhys was utterly confused. He looked toward Easton, who looked equally perplexed.

The rest had all assumed that because he could not feel, he would not be able to move either. It never occurred to them to ask him to try.

"What is involved in this operation?" Rhys asked.

"It would involve opening the leg in the position of the break to see if it was set properly. If we can discover a bone fragment, or something like, that is affecting the nerves, then we can remove it."

"Is this procedure actually possible? On the battlefield, it was common knowledge that surgeons could do no more than amputate," Rhys recalled.

"I will be frank. There have not been many successful operations. It is a verra new area of discovery. And there is always a chance of infection, though I am an advocate of the theories of antisepsis by Sir John Pringle and Bernard Courtois. It would be up to you to determine if it is worth the risk. If you choose not to operate, there is slim chance that you will recover movement of your entire leg. But the longer you delay, the more likely the damage to the nerves will be permanent."

"How long will this operation take? It sounds quite tedious," Elinor asked, engrossed in the conversation.

"That is still the greatest limitation," the surgeon explained. "We have no effective means of anaesthesia, so we are limited in time and tolerance of the patient."

"I sought him out, because he was the best surgeon I worked with in the field. He is much more proficient and timely than myself," Dr. Craig said reassuringly to Rhys.

Rhys nodded. "It seems there is no other choice. I either accept being a cripple, or I take the chance."

The surgeon agreed. "I will need to set up an operating room. I would like to commence as soon as possible in order to minimize any further damage."

The doctors left along with Elinor, Seamus and Easton in order to see to the preparations. Beatrice remained in the room with Rhys.

Beatrice walked over to his bedside. "Would you prefer to be alone?" He looked her in the eye and shook his head. She took his hand and sat next to him for the duration of his wait. He had accepted her presence, and this was not the time for words.

Dr. Craig entered the room to retrieve Rhys for the operation. He glanced at them holding hands but said nothing.

"Shall we?" Dr. Craig asked Rhys, "Do you have any more questions?"

"How much whisky have you? I do not scruple to confess I need the liquid courage," Rhys confessed.

"Nonsense. It is one situation where more is better. Then whisky is to be your drug of choice?"

"That, and a good swoon." They all chuckled. "I prefer it to the laudanum. Nasty stuff." He shrivelled up his face with disgust.

"Verra well. Here is a cordial Lady Easton thought would help with pain." He handed him a glass.

"God bless her," Rhys said gratefully. "What is in this?" Rhys sniffed the concoction sceptically.

"I believe she said it is valerian and brewed wild cherries. She said they used it in America to help with the pains of childbirth. She also said if you use it all, you may go pick more when it is her time."

"I would be much obliged." More than they could imagine.

"I imagine the worst part will be the opening of the leg. There will be some time when the surgeon is searching the wound when it should not be as painful," Dr. Craig began.

Rhys held up his hand to stop the doctor. He did not want the grotesque visual images. "Pray, leave the details to yourself. I think I would prefer to find my tolerance with a nice Highland whisky."

Easton knocked on the door. "Did someone say single malt? I have come to the rescue," he said in his best deep voice as he strode into the room carrying the whisky decanter. He took a swig, then handed the rest of the bottle to Rhys.

"That's a very fine whisky your brother makes there, Craig," Vernon said appreciatively as he eyed the decanter longingly.

Rhys promptly took a big long drink and tucked the bottle under his arm out of Easton's reach. "Not bad at all," Rhys concurred.

Dr. Craig chuckled. "Shall we?" The two men began to assist Rhys out of bed.

Beatrice squeezed Rhys's hand reassuringly, "I will be here when it is over."

Before they lifted him, his mother and Aunt Mary knocked and were waiting at the doorway with Catriona.

"The children have made you some notes, Rhys." His aunt Mary stepped forward and showed him their handiwork. She nodded to Catriona, who stepped up and handed Rhys a doll her mother had given her.

"This is my favourite doll, Master. She will protect you and keep you from being afraid. Just hug her tight if you get scared. It works when I miss my mama," the little girl explained.

Rhys reached out and took the doll. He held out his hand to her and she took it. He gave the doll a hug and said to Catriona, "I will take good care of her for you. But I am so glad you shared with me because I was afraid."

Catriona smiled and nodded knowingly. She watched him being carried off with the doll and looked like she was having second thoughts about parting with it. Beatrice came up beside her and gave her a hug. "That was very selfless and brave of you Catriona."

"So what shall we do now?" Catriona asked.

"I am going to wear holes in the carpet," Beatrice admitted.

Beatrice was wishing she could become her mother or Mrs. Bennet right now and have a fit of the vapours. She had heard of salons being all the rage in London where they did such. She was fairly certain anything would be better than waiting another minute longer. She had already taken a walk, said prayers at the chapel, taken tea, read a story to the children, and still there was no word about Rhys.

Everyone had gathered in the parlour waiting for news, growing more anxious by the moment.

"What could be taking so long?" Beatrice asked in frustration. "I understood surgery to be a quick process."

Easton answered, "It cannot be a good sign. The soldiers would beg for the fastest surgeons on the battlefield because of the torture. The longer the surgeon took, the worse the pain."

"Easton, that is decidedly unhelpful at the moment," Beatrice chastised.

The men began debating why no one had yet discovered a means of anaesthesia, when Dr. Craig finally entered the parlour.

"How is he, Doctor?" the Countess asked first.

"He slept through most of the procedure. Whatever cordial Lady Easton used, it worked like magic."

"Thank God," Beatrice said, relieved. That had been her gravest concern. "Do you think the operation successful?"

"I am uncertain at this point. When he awakens, we will ken better. The surgeon did find a bone fragment from the break that he believes to be the culprit. The main question is how much of the damage is irreversible."

"Does that mean the operation may not have helped?" the Countess asked.

"That is exactly what it means, I am afraid," he said frankly, "but at least now there is a chance."

"Thank you, Dr. Craig." Several of them echoed their gratitude.

Beatrice left the gathering in the parlour and decided to wait upstairs for Rhys to wake up. She knocked gently and entered the apartment. Elinor and Easton were holding vigil with the patient.

"Any changes?" Beatrice asked hopefully.

Elinor shook her head. "No, I am afraid he might sleep a while. The mixture of whisky with the cordial and pure exhaustion from the experience can knock them out for some time."

"That makes sense. I have had neither whisky nor a cordial, but I am exhausted from the experience." She looked toward Elinor with sympathy. "I am certain you must be beyond yourself, Elly. You should rest, and I will stay with him. If he is to be like this for some time, then you must relax when you can."

Easton agreed. "I hope my wife will listen to you because she needs to rest more in her final month."

She had a whole month left to go? Beatrice was bewildered. She did not think Elinor could grow any larger without bursting. She kept that thought to herself. Easton helped his wife to her feet. Elinor rubbed her back with a grimace on her face.

"Are you all right?" Beatrice asked with concern.

"I am persuaded I will be fine. I stood much during the operation which must be why my back aches. Nothing a nice hot bath will not cure," Elinor tried to reassure Easton and Beatrice.

"Please get some rest and take care of yourself. I am so grateful you are here, but you must also consider your little one." Beatrice could not help but glance at Elinor's stomach. It looked like she was growing an army in there.

The two of them left, Elinor waddling her way out. Beatrice watched them leave and wondered if she would ever be a mother. She had never given much consideration to what that entailed, but she knew she was supposed to produce heirs. Now, that would not matter so much.

Beatrice made herself comfortable in the chair beside Rhys's bed. She watched the evening sun move behind the mountain, emitting a deep pink hue across the horizon. She felt peaceful watching Rhys sleep. She knew her time with him was limited. She would either marry Dr. Craig, or return to London soon. She felt like the friendship was healing between her and Rhys, and that was more than she had hoped for previously.

Beatrice said a quick prayer of thanks for that, and for the operation going well. She prayed that he would be able to walk again and that there would be no infection. She grew drowsy as she sat in the chair and watched the sun set.

CHAPTER 18

*B*eatrice awoke with a start when she felt a hand on her arm. The room was dark and she was disorientated.

"Shh. It's all right, lass," The voice said soothingly. "It is only me, lass. I have come to check on Lord Vernon."

He lit a taper and set it on the night stand. Beatrice stood and stretched. Chairs were deuced uncomfortable to sleep in. She shivered, rubbing her hands up and down her arms. She walked over to the window and pulled it closed. The nights were growing colder as autumn neared.

"What time is it?" Beatrice asked through a yawn.

"'Tis near midnight. I am staying the night so I can be here when he awakens. I wanted to look in on him again before I retired."

Beatrice nodded. "He has not been awake to my knowledge. I heard him groan a little earlier, but he went right back to sleep."

"I will try to wake him. If he has nothing for pain now, he will be miserable later," the doctor explained.

"Lord Vernon?" Dr. Craig put his hand on his shoulder and gently shook.

Rhys moved a little but did not wake up. Dr. Craig called his name louder and shook him again. Rhys's eyes opened but he seemed unable to focus, so the doctor moved into Rhys's line of vision and spoke to him again, "Lord Vernon, can you hear me? It's Dr. Craig. I have come to see how you are faring. Can you tell me how you are feeling?"

Rhys shook his head as if to clear the fog. "Aye, I can hear you, but my head is spinning." He put his head back down and closed his eyes.

"'Tis most likely the effects of the whisky with the herbs. May I examine you before we let you rest?"

Rhys nodded his assent but did not open his eyes.

Dr. Craig pulled back the covers, and Beatrice had to turn away from the sight of his leg. There was a long incision with sutures, and it made her stomach queasy to look at it.

The doctor began touching the leg and asking Rhys if he could feel it. A few times Rhys said yes, and a few times his face twisted. "It is as if I can feel something but it is not right." Rhys's brow furrowed as he searched for the right description, "Perhaps numbness? But not quite."

"That is a verra good sign. There is much improvement already. Can you move your toes?"

Rhys wiggled them in response. "Excellent," Dr. Craig said excitedly.

"Can you bend your leg at all?"

Rhys made a small movement with his leg but yelped in pain.

"That is enough for now. You were unable to do that this morning. I will let you go back to sleep, but you best take something for the pain first."

Beatrice handed him the cordial she had prepared while Dr. Craig was examining Rhys.

Rhys complied and promptly went back to sleep. Dr. Craig turned toward Beatrice and said, "Why do I not stay with him for now. You need to get some rest."

Beatrice just nodded. She did not even have enough energy to argue. "Good night then, Gavin."

"Good night, Beatrice."

~

The next day brought much rejoicing. Dr. Murray was pleased with the outcome of the operation. Even though Rhys had not recovered full feeling, he did have the ability to move his leg. The doctor said there was a small chance that the rest of his feeling might return, but it was more likely the damage would be permanent. He did anticipate Rhys would be able to walk again with a limp.

Dr. Murray was leaving to return to Edinburgh, so Dr. Craig said they would need to be judicious in cleaning the incision to keep infection out and from ruining all of their progress. The valet was assisting Dr. Craig and Seamus with all of Rhys's care, so Beatrice stayed out of their way. She felt like she had done what she needed to do. Truly, she did not have the constitution for nursing.

She was sullen. The time had come for her to make a decision. But first, she was anxious to know how her cousin was doing, so she chose to check on her and delay her decisions.

Beatrice made her way to Easton and Elly's apartments. She knocked on the door and heard a groan.

"Elinor? It is Beatrice. Are you well?" Beatrice asked, concerned.

"Never better! Do you think you could help me?"

Beatrice walked into the room and looked around.

"Behind the screen," Elinor replied with a strained voice.

Beatrice looked, and Elinor was wrapped in a towel bent over the side of the bath-tub.

"Whatever is the matter? What can I do?" Beatrice rushed over to Elly's side.

"First, please help me to the bed. Second, please send for the doctor if he is still here. I believe the baby is coming," Elinor said calmly.

"Is it not too early?" Beatrice asked worriedly.

"I have no control over that." Elinor smiled through gritted teeth. As Beatrice helped her walk over to the bed, another labour pain hit Elinor, and she bent over and started breathing heavily.

"What shall I do now?" Beatrice did not like being so ignorant about this.

"Be still." Elinor kept breathing strangely, and then she stood back up, relieved of the pains besetting her, and proceeded to the bed.

"Are you sure you will be all right while I find Dr. Craig? Where is Easton?"

"I will be fine. I would prefer you find Dr. Craig first." She smiled. Beatrice nodded and ran as fast as she could.

Of course, he was nowhere to be found. She looked in Rhys's apartments, but no one was there. She checked the study and parlour and finally found Lady Mary. She explained the situation, and Lady Mary rushed to be with Elinor while Beatrice searched for the men.

She found them by the stables, of all places. She could see them as she walked from the house. They had fashioned some poles out of wood for Rhys to practice standing with. Dr. Craig demonstrated how Rhys could even walk with them if he held his injured leg up.

"I am exhausted," Rhys exclaimed, "but it is a welcome exhausted."

"I am extremely pleased with your progress, Lord Vernon," Dr. Craig said. "That is enough for now. We can advance more later as you regain strength."

"You are a tough taskmaster, Doctor," Rhys said as he sat back down in the old Earl's Bath chair so they could roll him to the house.

"I am sorry to interrupt," Beatrice said breathlessly, "but Lord Easton and Dr. Craig are needed in Lady Easton's room. She was having labour pains when I left her and asked me to find you."

Dr. Craig nodded and asked Beatrice to see Lord Vernon back to the house. Easton had already started running.

Beatrice started laughing. "It certainly seems like we are keeping the doctor gainfully employed here. You should consider taking him on permanently, Rhys."

"Indeed. It seems I owe him my life and my future ability to walk."

Beatrice looked away. She tried to feel happiness for Rhys, and she did, but she also felt sad that she would no longer be a part of his life. It was impossible to only consider him as a friend, though she was thankful that they seemed to have achieved that again.

She wheeled Rhys back toward the house. She was not ready to go inside. She excused herself after seeing Rhys into the hands of his man and walked toward the river. She would return and help shortly, but she knew nothing of childbirth, and she desperately needed some fresh air and time to think.

She walked aimlessly and found herself at the pier. She had not intended to walk so far. She thought about the last time she was there with Dr. Craig. What a worthy man he was. She cared for him deeply, but Rhys was correct; she was not made for being a doctor's wife. She also knew in her heart that she did not love him, and she did not feel right about marrying him feeling thus.

Marriages of convenience were commonplace amongst the *ton*, but she knew that Gavin deserved to love and to be loved. Beatrice did not know if she could ever bring herself to marry another. She knew her parents would not be pleased, certainly her mother. Equally, she doubted her father anticipated the lesson, but she had discovered there was more to life than a prestigious marriage and wealth. She did not look forward to the conversation with Gavin, but she did not think he would be surprised.

Beatrice soaked in the beautiful scenery: the leaves beginning to change their colours. She would miss this place more than she ever imagined. She knew in her heart it was time to leave; she would ask Easton and Elly if she might accompany them when they returned home. That could be a while, she thought. *The baby!* She had completely lost track of time. She had best get back.

"Where have you been?" Lady Mary asked hurriedly when she saw Beatrice.

Beatrice replied, "I took a walk and lost track of time. I did not think myself useful here."

"Never mind, we need your help now."

"Has something happened?"

"The babies have happened," she exclaimed.

"Babies? *As in more than one?*"

Lady Mary nodded and led her into the sitting room adjoining the bedroom. She was promptly handed a little bundle and Beatrice stared at it, alarmed. She had never held a baby, let alone a new-born.

"Cuddle her to you," Lady Mary instructed and helped her find the right position. "You will not hurt her." Beatrice did as she was told, but was still terrified. She sat down in a chair with the baby and felt a little bit safer. She looked around and noticed the Earl and Sir Charles sitting and holding bundles themselves.

Beatrice made an indelicate noise. *"There are three?"*

Both men nodded their heads with smiles from ear to ear.

"I am holding Gareth Maximus," the Earl said proudly.

"And I am holding Charles Andrew," Sir Charles pronounced.

"Who am I holding?" Beatrice asked. She thought Lady Mary had said she was a girl. The men looked at each other and Sir Charles said, "I think Elly would like to tell you her name." Lady Mary spoke up, "We may see if Lady Easton is ready for visitors." They crossed the room and Lady Mary knocked gently on the door. The door was opened by a grinning Easton.

He saw Beatrice and welcomed her in. "Elly has been waiting to speak with you."

Beatrice was surprised. She looked to Lady Mary to take the baby from her but Easton stopped her. "No, please bring her with you."

Beatrice stood gingerly holding the baby. She was afraid she might drop her, but she managed without any mishap. She followed Easton to Elinor's bedside.

"There you are," Elinor exclaimed.

"I hear congratulations are in order...*three* times?" She still could not believe Elinor had just given birth to three babies. "I did not realize I was needed, or I would not have stayed away so long. I have no experience with these things," she said, embarrassed.

"That is not why we were looking for you. We wished to ask if you would consent to be her godmother. We would like to name her Elizabeth Beatrice."

It took a moment for her to register their words. She immediately started and handed Elinor the baby and shook her head emphatically. "I am wholly undeserving of such an honour. I cannot believe you would even consider such."

Elinor reached out for Beatrice's hand. "I disagree. I cannot think of anyone else I would rather my daughter be named after. Most would not have handled your situation so gracefully. I must admit I was not sure you would comprehend you had done wrong, or that you would be willing to change. I would be thrilled if my daughter had such strength of character. We would be honoured for you to play an important role in her life."

Beatrice struggled for words. "I do not know what to say. I do not know how to be a godmother."

"And I do not know how to be a mother, but we will learn together. I have a feeling we will need all the help we can find." She looked to Easton as if still unable to believe they had three babies.

Help came from an unexpected source. The Dowager Duchess arrived in short order when she heard Elinor had been delivered of triplets, complete with an entourage of servants she deemed necessary to her comfort and that of Elinor. Beatrice could not but laugh when her tiny grandmother set the house on its ear with her arrival.

No one who was familiar with the Dowager could mistake who had descended upon the house. Beatrice heard the familiar voice and was unsure how she felt about seeing her grandmother again. She knew the Dowager had never cared for her or her mother. If Beatrice chose to re-enter Society, she would need her grandmother's approval. She did not know if her grandmother would forgive her for her acts against Elinor, but she would likely be willing to support her against the Duchess if she felt it to her advantage.

Beatrice had ensconced herself in nursery duty, there not being a plethora of nurses in remote Scotland. She was taking her new role as godmother very seriously, and was trying to alleviate some of the work for Elinor. They had all learned to change nappies; they had all discovered which baby was most likely to have wind; they had all taken turns on night duty. She would not have admitted to herself that she welcomed the distraction, but she had scarcely seen either Rhys or Gavin since the arrival of the babies.

The Dowager had thought of the need for nurses, however, and brought a surfeit of them for the babies' every need. Beatrice found herself relieved of her duty and instantly commanded to appear before her grandmother. She made her way to the sitting room that the matron of the family had chosen as her personal boudoir, wondering why she would choose now for a cose with her when she had never bothered before.

Beatrice entered the room and made a curtsy to the Dowager. "Good day, Grandmother. I trust you had a pleasant journey."

"Let me have a good look at you before we chat. I am credibly informed that I shall be shocked at your appearance." The old lady surveyed Beatrice through her quizzing glass, scanning her from head to boot. Beatrice stood obediently allowing this demeaning impertinence, awaiting the diatribe she knew to be coming. Instead, a look of humour crept into the eyes of the lady. "It is astonishing how well you look now you are out from under Willy's thumb!"

Beatrice cringed inwardly at the Dowager's pet name for her mother. She called her that at every opportunity to irritate her.

The Dowager patted the seat next to her on the sofa. "Come sit and tell me about things here. Then I will give you the letter your father sent for you."

"I am not sure what you would wish to know. I have been spending my time caring for children, which must shock your deepest sensibilities."

"Consider me astonished. Carry on." She waved this old news away dismissively.

"Rhys was injured and is learning to walk again," Beatrice continued.

"Yes, I did hear that. That is why Elly got this hare-brained scheme to deliver her babies in the wild!"

171

"You may blame me for that. I never dreamed she would think to come in person!"

"Andrew tells me you are to marry the doctor. I collect your mother knows nothing of this?" the Dowager said with a grin. "I hear he is rather fetching."

Beatrice shook her head, not wanting to answer this line of questioning.

"What of Rhys? The betrothal is off between him and Lady Margaux." She narrowed her gaze into an eagle-eyed stare. "And no pretending you do not understand my meaning!"

Beatrice knew that look and struggled not to squirm under the scrutiny. She sighed. "We have achieved a friendship again. But he was prepared to marry another, Grandmother. I have come to accept his feelings, but I do not know if marriage to another is what is best for me."

The Dowager remained silent for a moment. "You plan to stay here indefinitely?"

"I do not yet know. I must decide soon."

"I best give you the letter from your father, then. I will allow you some privacy." The Dowager rose and retrieved a letter from her sitting room and handed it to Beatrice. She gave her a pat on the shoulder before leaving the room. Beatrice stared after her before breaking the seal. Receiving approbation from her grandmother was unsettling. She let out a sigh and opened the letter.

Beatrice,

I implore you to return to London as soon as you are able. Napoleon has been defeated at Waterloo, but there has been no word from Nathaniel. The English sustained heavy losses, especially Nathaniel's regiment. I have sent some men to investigate his whereabouts until he is found. The Duchess is beside herself and wants you to return immediately. I, too, would enjoy your presence at this most distressing time. The offer still stands for the children.

Your loving,

Papa

Beatrice felt an ache in her heart at the possibility of Nathaniel's death. Much had happened since the last day she saw him. He had been right about her, and she had been churlish. Never was one so cross as when they knew they were in the wrong, much to her shame. Even though she did not condone what he had done to Elinor, she knew in her heart that he was changed—as she was. Elinor had assured her that she had forgiven him, and so Beatrice would try to do the same. She had already decided to depart, and this was the final assurance that she needed to go.

CHAPTER 19

The time for leaving was here. It was growing colder, and the leaves were changing. Elinor felt that the babies were old enough to be moved. It was astonishing the change three new-borns wrought upon a household. Twenty older children in the orphanage had not produced the upheaval that these three had. Beatrice thought it likely due to their propensity to sleep during the day and be awake at night.

Beatrice was much altered by the priory; she grew apprehensive about life in London. Naturally her relationship with her mother would be strained. She had not yet formed a scheme to soothe the lady's delicate nerves.

Rhys was making a miraculous recovery. He still did not have complete feeling in his leg, but he was able to hobble around remarkably well with his crutches. Gavin said when the break was fully healed that he could begin to put weight on the leg again.

The morning was cool and misty. The loch was eerie with fog rising from it; Beatrice could scarcely make out the mountain behind it. Beatrice had asked Gavin to meet her at the pier this morning. She needed to let him know she was returning to London. They had not grown any closer since Rhys's accident, and she suspected that Gavin knew where her heart lay.

"Guid morning, Beatrice," Gavin said as he walked toward her. "I hope I have not kept you waiting long."

"Not at all. I enjoy the serenity," she smiled at him.

"Aye. Scotland has that effect on me too."

She was not sure how to break the news to him, so she said bluntly, "Gavin, I wanted to let you know I am leaving for London." She paused. "For good."

He put his hands in his pockets and blew out some air through pursed lips. "I ken it was coming, lass, I just dinna expect it to be so soon." He paused. "I selfishly hoped that I would be able to change your mind. But I have been busy and unable to court you properly."

Beatrice shook her head, and a tear fell down her cheek. "Please do not think this has anything to do with you. I could not make you more perfect if I tried."

"Then what can I say? What can I do?" he asked desperately.

"You can find the person that will love you as you deserve. If my heart had not been given away eleven years ago, it would be yours."

She held out her arms to him, and he reached out and embraced her. She could not stop the sobs that came. She hoped he would understand that she could not help loving love Rhys, even if she could not have him.

"He's a good man. And a verra lucky one."

"Lucky to have you, Gavin. He would not be here without you."

He nodded in appreciation for her comment and kissed her on the head before turning and walking away.

Beatrice watched him leave and wrapped her arms around herself. She knew she had made the right decision, but why must it hurt so much?

Rhys was in a temper. Beatrice had been toying with his affections again, and he needed to vent some frustrations. She would not leave his side when he begged her to, and now she was playing least in sight when he most wanted her around. She used the babies as pretence; she expected him to believe she had discovered a maternal inclination overnight?

He was left to look at her pretty doctor several times a day when required to do his bloody exercise regime. He owed Dr. Adonis his life and he wanted nothing more than to draw his cork. That spoke volumes about his current state of mind. He needed a good round at Jackson's, or a long hard ride, neither of which were options in his crippled state. If he didn't do something manly and sweaty soon, he would burst.

He sent his man to find Easton. He would understand. They could borrow the old Earl's Bath chair and steal away for some shooting. Surely there could be no harm in that. If he could shoot from a horse he could shoot from a chair. He could not bear to be around the brawny Scottish doctor and his breathtakingly blue eyes and delicious burr at the moment. He shuddered with distaste as he recollected the descriptions he heard the silly females spewing about Dr. Craig. The worst part was that he liked the doctor. His melancholy deepened knowing he was losing his love to a better man.

Easton arrived and was more than happy to oblige the request. He retrieved the Bath chair and they stole out of the house with bows, rifles and hunters in tow. Rhys giggled like a schoolgirl as they made their way across the property. He felt an exhilarating burst of freedom from his small act of defiance.

Easton adjusted targets and they prepared to shoot. As Rhys pulled on his string...

"Guid morning," the deep Scottish brogue said more solemnly than usual.

Rhys swallowed the bile that rose in his throat as he released the arrow to sail right past the target.

"Missed the mark," Easton teased.

"Nay, he missed the target," Dr. Craig corrected.

With difficulty Rhys refrained from snapping back an acid retort.

"Why not join us?" Easton offered, with a gleam of mockery in his eyes.

"I am a bit rusty, but I could use a diversion," Gavin said meekly.

Dr. Craig stepped up, pulled the string back and hit the target dead centre. Rhys was obliged to own that was a decent shot. Easton handed Rhys another arrow. He bent over and whispered in Rhys's ear, "Imagine his face in the centre."

Rhys pulled back on the string and the arrow sliced Dr. Craig's in two.

Easton let out a low whistle and handed the doctor another arrow, enjoying every moment.

"Verra nice, Lord Vernon."

Rhys gave a nod of his head and waited for the doctor to have his turn. It would be easier to hate him if he weren't such a gentleman.

"You should try to shoot standing. That would be good exercise for your leg today. I ken you wish to return to London soon, so we best have you walking," the doctor said with a slight sardonic smile lurking about his eyes.

Rhys mumbled under his breath, "Wants me away from Bea, the blasted poacher." He took another arrow from Easton.

"Swallow your spleen, old man," Easton whispered.

Perhaps Rhys had not mumbled as much as he thought. He stood and took aim, hitting the mark again.

"She is going back to London," Gavin said quietly as he took his turn.

"Beg pardon?" Rhys was stunned.

Gavin turned and looked Rhys straight in the eye, before handing his bow to Easton and walking away.

Beatrice spent the next few days preparing to leave. The Douglas children had decided they would remain at the priory. The girls had become attached to the Millbanks while Beatrice was helping care for

Rhys. Seamus wanted to stay close to Gavin, so he was to attend a school in Dumfries so he could visit his sisters often.

Beatrice was sorrowful that she would not see Catriona and Maili every day, but she did think it best to keep the children together. She was sure to let them know they always had a place with her. They had already found a new governess, so she was not needed any longer.

Lady Vernon and Lady Mary would stay to continue helping Rhys until he could tolerate the journey to London. She had spoken to him very little since his operation. She decided it was best to keep her distance, thinking it easier to leave that way. The Countess appeared to have declared a truce. She seemed to have decided that Beatrice was sincere and was no longer a threat to marrying her son.

There was so much to celebrate and be grateful for that Beatrice was frustrated with herself for her melancholy. Rhys was recovering, and the triplets were healthy. She wished circumstances had been otherwise with Gavin, but she felt it best to be honest now.

She shut the lid to the trunk she had finished packing. She still had her small portmanteau, which she meant to keep as a reminder of this journey. She took her caped pelisse and headed out to walk one last time. She walked through the park toward the loch, turning things over and over in her mind.

Beatrice watched as one red leaf fell slowly from the top of a tree. It was as if it was suspended in the air. It was fascinating how some fell quickly, but this one lingered as it made its way toward the ground, reluctant to fall. She could relate to the leaf suspended, yet falling and not knowing where to land. She held out her hand trying to provide a landing spot for it.

"They never land on your hand for some reason," Rhys spoke behind her.

She kept her hand out waiting for the leaf to land. Her heart began to race with him so near. She wished he did not have this effect on her, but it had been this way for eleven years; he would probably always control her heart.

"How are you feeling? This is a long way to walk."

"My leg will not ever be the same; I will always limp. And I will certainly not enjoy the winter now," Rhys jested.

"I suppose you best make haste southward." A gust of wind blew the leaf away, missing her hand. She turned to face him.

"Aye. I heard you were leaving soon," Rhys spoke quietly.

"Have you come to forcibly remove me?" she teased. It did feel good to be on easy terms again.

"I would prefer to have you stay willingly," he said earnestly. "When Dr. Craig told me you were leaving, I thought I would foolishly come throw myself at your feet. Though not literally." He laughed nervously. "Will you give me another chance? I am wretched without you."

Was she hearing him properly? Could he still love her? She had all but given up.

"Unless, of course, you are wholly indifferent. I never stopped loving you, Bea. Is there any hope left for me?"

"You would still have me?" She could not believe what she was hearing.

"I thought that horrid day in January when you did not answer, that you preferred exile to me. Every day without you has been torture." He poked at a leaf with his crutch.

"I was too ashamed to answer you, Rhys. I was jealous of the attention you paid Elinor. And when I discovered Elly had been violated, and I had worsened her pain, I could not bear myself. As horrible as losing you was, I needed to lose you. *Ton* life had become a ridiculous game. Others were not actually people to me any more. I had let you down, and my pride was bruised." Tears trickled down her face.

Rhys hobbled closer. "I was afraid I had lost you for good, Bea. I was ready to throw my life away with someone I did not love."

Beatrice understood. "And while I care deeply for Gavin, Rhys, you own my heart. You always have."

Rhys was too choked to speak, but took her in his arms.

"So where do we go from here?" Beatrice asked.

"Down the aisle? We happen to be at a priory." He gestured toward

179

the old church. "On second thoughts, we are in Scotland we do not need an aisle, or a licence, or anyone's consent," he pronounced.

"You want to marry now? Do we not need to start again? Were you not the one who jilted me?"

He cleared his throat. "Very well. Forgive me for not going down on bended knee. Beatrice Wilhelmina Chalcroft, whom I have loved since you were nine years old and poured slime on me, who is afraid of animals and grotesque hairy body parts. Who paints atrociously, but has me so enchanted I think it a masterpiece. Who understands my ill sense of humour. Who forces her way into my room to care for me against my wishes. Who has the most stunning hazel eyes and auburn locks I have ever seen. Who sets my soul on fire with her brilliant smile. Who knows me better than I know myself. Who has been my best friend forever and always. Who will say, yes, Rhys, I would like nothing better than to marry you right at this moment." He cast her a brilliant smile. Beatrice was speechless. And she was a watering pot.

"I ought to have planned this better," he said thoughtfully as he tried to balance on one leg and hand her his handkerchief.

Beatrice tried not to laugh, but her lips quivered despite the tears.

"How about this then," Rhys quoted in his best Scottish accent,

O my luve is like a red, red rose,
That's newly sprung in June:
O my luve is like the melodie,
That's sweetly played in tune.
As fair art thou, my bonnie lass,
So deep in luve am I;
And I will luve thee still, my dear,
Till a` the seas gang dry.
Till a` the seas gang dry, my dear,
And the rocks melt wi` the sun;
And I will luve thee still my dear,
While the sands o` life shall run.

. . .

"Robert Burns. That is a nice touch." Beatrice was impressed. "But would have had more effect in a kilt."

He shoved his crutches under one arm and used his free hand to caress her cheek and pull her face to his. He brushed his lips across hers. She stood there waiting for more.

He pulled his head back and shook it as he said, "Eh, eh, eh. Not until you answer."

She reached up and pulled his head back down to hers. That was how a kiss should make you feel.

When they stopped for breath, she asked, "How is that for an answer?"

"I am unconvinced," he said smugly, eyes twinkling, his forehead against hers.

She repeated her answer more emphatically until he began to wobble. "Now?"

"That was more convincing." He took the ruby ring out of his pocket and slipped it onto her finger. "In fact, as far as I am concerned, that fulfils Scottish law for a wedding ceremony."

"Is there not supposed to be a witness?" She looked at him sceptically.

"Details, details."

She shook her head. "Let us get you back. You must be tired from being on your leg so long."

"It was worth it."

Beatrice helped Rhys make his way slowly back up the path to the house. She felt genuinely happy and at peace again. She tilted her head to the sky and said a quick prayer of thanks. She stopped suddenly.

"What is it?" Rhys asked worriedly.

"I would like to have my parents here."

Rhys groaned, "That will take forever."

"Maybe, but will not our mothers be thrilled?" she said sarcastically.

"You must tell them. I say we inform them after the fact."

She gave him a swift nudge with her elbow.

CHAPTER 20

*T*he day of the wedding was a cool, brisk autumn day in the lowlands. Mist was rising off the loch and the trees were glorious shades of gold, red and green. There was a dusting of snow on the mountain peak, as if blessing their union. Beatrice looked from the pier over the still waters and inhaled the air fresh with pine and smoke from the chimneys. Perfect.

She had escaped the frenzy of wedding preparations to calm her nerves. As the Countess and Duchess had drawn battle lines dividing the house, Rhys did not hesitate to remind her that they could have been married weeks ago, and inviting her parents was her idea. She was glad they were there, but she was uncertain how to best handle them yet. She was not necessary for the mothers' machinations anyway.

Once the arguing about following Scottish wedding traditions had ensued, Beatrice bowed out of the discussions. The days leading up to the wedding had been torture. Beatrice and Rhys had been alone without restrictions or rules for weeks, and then suddenly, add the Duchess back in to the picture and all of the old feelings began swarming inside her. Leave it to her mother to take the enjoyment out of her wedding. Thankfully the Duke had abided by Beatrice's wishes and not allowed the Duchess to invite all of Society. That would have ruined the day for her. Scotland and the priory were everything her old life was not. She was not sure how she would go on from here, but she knew with Rhys it would work.

Beatrice reluctantly made her way back to the house when she heard the bells chime the hour before the ceremony. Addie and her lady's maid from London, Jenny, came to help her dress. Beatrice had selected a simple cream gown—to the mortification of her mother—but she insisted. It was symbolic of the new Beatrice, as was making a stand with the Duchess. It was not much, but it was a start.

Jenny placed a simple blue ribbon around her forehead to pull her curls from her face and tie her veil in place. "Something blue."

Beatrice turned to look in the glass, but Addie stopped her. "No, ye canna look. It's verra bad luck," she chastised.

"But you look beautiful, milady. I think this new look suits you," Jenny said reassuringly.

"Me too, Jenny," Beatrice smiled. "It will certainly make your job easier."

"It is hard te believe ye are the same person who appeared at the back door last winter," Addie said. Lady Mary slipped into the room to wish the bride luck. "Here, put this in your slipper." Lady Mary handed the coin to Addie, who bent down to place the sixpence in Beatrice's shoe for luck.

"I never knew Scots were so superstitious. Between the grey horses, the heather in my bouquet, the lock of hair sewn in my hem, the veil...I know I am forgetting something. Oh, tying the girdle in knots. I am sure Lord Vernon will thank you for that later." Beatrice shook her head in dismay, trying not to blush.

"And don' forget te take his right hand at the altar," Addie reminded her.

A knock on the door brought the Duke in to greet his daughter. The women curtsied to his Grace and then hastened out of the room.

"You look beautiful, Bea. I could not be more proud of you," the Duke said as he leaned down to kiss his daughter's cheek. "I am only sad to give you away because I feel I am only now getting to know you. Promise you will make time for this old man once you are married."

"I promise. I would like nothing more." Beatrice reached up to return a kiss to her father's cheek as a tear rolled down her face.

The Duchess sailed into the room. "Robert, stop making her cry. She will have a red nose and blotches on her face," she scolded.

"Mother," Beatrice said calmly.

"I brought you the pearls that were given to me by my mother on my wedding day. This is not where I expected to be giving them to you, however, nor the wedding I anticipated at St. George's, but I suppose it will do," the Duchess said haughtily.

Beatrice was disappointed, but she knew she should not expect her mother to act any differently. She did not have any reason to change. If Beatrice had not been sent here, she would still be behaving just like her. Beatrice remained silent.

The Duke broke the silence, "I just came from Vernon. He looked a little weary from his blackening. I think they took it easily with him because of his injury."

"What is blackening?" Beatrice looked appalled. It did not sound pleasant at all.

"A Scottish tradition for men the night before the wedding. Nothing for you to worry over, my dear. Although, he might still be a bit sticky in places." The Duke chuckled. "He asked me to give you this." The Duke kissed her head and handed her a small package. "I will give you a few moments." He left, taking the Duchess with him.

Beatrice nodded as the Duke slipped out of the room, grateful for the moment of privacy. She held the small present. It was wrapped in velvet and tied with a ribbon, like she used to wrap her letters to him. She lifted it to her nose. He had not forgotten the lavender. Tears were flowing as she untied the ribbon. Inside was the most beautiful brooch she had ever seen: two silver hearts intertwined with a ruby heart at the centre. The back inscription read:

go deo mo chroí

. . .

Forever my Heart. She read the translation on the small paper Rhys had placed inside with the Scottish luckenbooth.

Instead of pinning the brooch to her dress, Beatrice wove the pearls through the clasp so it would hang near her heart. She was not sure she would ever remove it. She wiped the tears back from her face. Her body was shaking, and her stomach was tied in more knots than her girdle. Not from fear of wedding Rhys, but from fear of being the wife he deserved. Fear for being able to continue as her new self in Society. She should not be so nervous. She would be with Rhys and that would give her strength.

The Duke tapped on the door to see if she was ready. He guided her to the carriage led by the grey horses. The priory was too close to ride, but the Countess insisted on the tradition. Who was she to argue?

They stepped from the carriage into the old priory chapel, the place where Beatrice had come during her hopeless moments. The pews were filled with the orphans and her family. The only one missing was Nathaniel, and she felt a hole in her heart from his absence. She vowed to give him another chance if he lived. After all, if she had not been given a second chance, she would not be marrying Rhys today. She sent up a quick prayer for her brother and nodded to her father that she was ready. Bagpipes announced her entrance and accompanied her down the aisle.

She looked up toward Rhys as she continued down the small aisle, and almost burst into laughter as he stood proudly wearing a kilt. *She should have expected that.* Rhys threw a wink at her, as if reading her thoughts, and she smiled back, all the love in her heart showing through. She heard a gasp from the front pew. Let her mother be mortified at her behaviour, she would have to adjust.

The Duke presented Beatrice to Rhys, and she placed her right hand in his. Vicar Millbanks conducted the ceremony with Scottish wedding prayers:

Lord help us to remember when
We first met and the strong
love that grew between us.
To work that love into
practical things so that nothing
can divide us.
We ask for words both kind
and loving and hearts always
ready to ask forgiveness
as well as to forgive.
Dear Lord, we put our
marriage into your hands.

Ye are Blood of my Blood, and Bone of my Bone.
I give ye my Body, that we Two might be One.
I give ye my Spirit, 'til our Life shall be Done
Amen.

They each recited their vows, and Rhys placed a band on her finger next to the ruby ring. She looked down, a gold band of knots in a continuous circle, another Scottish tradition. As Rhys kissed her to seal their vows, it felt right. *Lady Vernon.* A new name for the new Beatrice.

EPILOGUE

*A*re you sure you want to do this?" Rhys looked her straight in the eye.

"I am as sure as I am ever going to be," Beatrice said nervously, "but I need to do this. Are you sure you are ready?"

"Absolutely, positively. I have been waiting for this day for months. Are you sure you remember what to do?"

Beatrice nodded unconvincingly. She had known ponies since she was small. She had no reason to be so afraid of them.

The groom handed Rhys the leading reins, and they began to walk toward the mounting blocks. "Remain calm and let her lead you. She has the best temperament of any horse I have ever met."

"I am glad of that, at least."

"Remember that horses can sense your emotion. If you are nervous, she will know that. If you trust her, she will trust you," he said reassuringly. He held out a lump of sugar to feed to his horse. "If that fails, bribery usually works."

Beatrice held out her hand to accept a piece. The last thing she wanted to do was have a horse bite her hand off, but this was part of conquering her fears. She held her palm out with the sugar to the horse and tried not to flinch as the large head with the enormous mouth and giant teeth descended towards her. The horse gently removed the sugar without touching her hand. Beatrice opened her eyes when she recognized she had been closing them. The mare nudged her hand looking for more.

Rhys whispered, "This would be a good time to pat her, and talk to her so she recognizes the sound of your voice."

She tentatively put her hand to the mare's forehead and rubbed gently. The horse nuzzled closer. "Good day, my lady. I am Beatrice."

"I believe she likes you. Shall we begin?" Rhys appeared about to burst with excitement.

Rhys helped Beatrice into her saddle. After he had her settled, Rhys pulled himself up onto his own horse rather gracefully, considering the injury he had suffered a few months ago. Beatrice saw him wince slightly as he lifted his injured leg over the horse, but he was so excited to ride again that she looked away as if she had not noticed.

"Promise you will not let go."

"I promise."

They made their way slowly down the path, both adjusting to the sensation. Beatrice was riding astride as her cousin Elinor had recommended for her to become more comfortable. Elinor had sent her a riding costume that split into a skirt for each leg. Beatrice thought it would be acceptable to ride that way on their own property away from town. She desperately wanted to conquer her fear and try something that was so important to Rhys.

As they rode slowly, and she realized the horse was gentle, she allowed herself to slowly relax. She looked over toward Rhys, who had a smile as wide as his face.

"I need not ask if you are enjoying yourself." She laughed.

"I do not think I could be happier. I did not want you to ride just for me, but I confess I am most happy to share another one of my favourite things with you." He winked.

Beatrice blushed at his implication.

They made their way slowly across their new property. After their wedding, the entire family had removed to Belgium to search for Nathaniel, and they had decided to purchase an estate in the south of

France for Rhys to have a warm place to winter. Now that Napoleon was defeated, it was possible to once again enjoy the Continent safely.

As Beatrice's comfort on the mare increased, she was able to appreciate the feel of the breeze in her face and the grace of the animal beneath her. They reached the edge of their property before she knew it. She had become so engrossed in the moment; she was unaware of how long they had been riding. She had actually been able to relax on a horse!

They pulled the horses to a stop and gazed out at the beauty before them. There were not adequate words to describe the emotions she felt. Above all, she felt grateful for the second chances they had both been given. Rhys dismounted and helped her slide off her horse. They stood together at the edge of the cliff in silent wonder, and the horses wandered to graze.

Rhys inhaled a deep breath. "Now *this* is how to do winter. In fact, you will have to work hard to convince me ever to winter in England again."

"Perhaps Christmas sometimes. I want our children to experience the magic of snow."

Rhys grimaced with distaste.

"It does not feel like Christmas this year. It is so warm, and Nathaniel..."

"I know, love, I know." Rhys kissed the top of her head and pulled her close. "We have to make new memories now."

The waves splashed gently against the rocks in the steep calanaques below. The view was a breath-taking panorama of limestone cliffs and crystal-clear blue waters. As she looked back toward the château perched atop the vineyard-covered hills, she felt a tear of appreciation roll down her cheek.

Rhys bent over and kissed the tear. "Please tell me that is a tear of happiness."

"I cannot believe you have to ask." She turned to gaze into his eyes.

"A wise man told me once, never try to understand a woman."

"The odious wretch. I am perfectly understandable."

Rhys tried to maintain a straight face; the solemnity was betrayed by the tiny muscle upturned at the corner of his mouth and the sparkle in his eye.

"Very well, I might have occasional moods. I must warn you; I am told they might get more severe over the next few months." Beatrice let the implication of her words sink in.

It did not take long. He pulled her into his arms and expressed his emotions in a kiss. "I suppose I can tolerate them for the cause."

"You have little choice."

"I will take you however I can have you, Bea. I saw what life was like without you, and I choose you. In any mood."

"You do tolerate my mother better than anyone else."

"That is simple. Treat her like a Duchess, smile, and agree with everything she says."

"Beast," she elbowed him playfully.

"And I am all yours."

"Shall we start back? Is your leg paining you?"

"I'll just say I am grateful we did not gallop. But we had best go. At our tortoise's pace, the hare will be awaking from his nap soon, and I do believe the Duchess is expecting us for Christmas dinner."

PREVIEW OF SEEKING REDEMPTION

LONDON, 1808

*N*athaniel woke, disorientated, to a dark room. His head was spinning, his mouth was dry, and he felt like the contents of his stomach would be expelled at any moment. He tried to lift his head to see where he was, but his eyes could not focus. This had been happening too often lately, waking up with a horrid headache in an unknown location. He squinted in the dim room, the only hint of light coming from the dying embers in the hearth. The room looked familiar, as if it were his father's house, not the rooms he kept.

Nathaniel rolled over and felt a leg. A lady's leg, by the feel of it, or more likely, a courtesan's. He looked down and noticed his clothing around his ankles. It was too bad he could not remember, he thought. That, too, had been happening often lately. He glanced at the lady's face to see if he recognized her. It was embarrassing not to remember these things when they met in the *ton's* drawing rooms. Ladies did not care for that.

He stumbled off the bed as he pulled his breeches up and tried to get a closer look. His head pounded and ached like never before. Perhaps he should take it easier on the opium pipe, or the whisky, he thought. He noticed the torn dress and golden curls. Strange, he did

191

not remember having a propensity toward roughness before. He scrunched up his face. There was an odd familiarity about this female.

As he pushed back the hair from her face, he noticed the scratches all over his arms. Then he saw her face.

Nathaniel broke out in a cold sweat all over as the reality of what he had done sobered him. He immediately started retching and shaking, emptying his stomach contents until he could only heave. He sat on to the floor next to the chamber pot. How could he have done such a thing? He concentrated but could not remember any of it. Maybe there had been something else in the pipe. He shook his head. *Oh God, oh God, oh God. What do I do now?*

He rose and made his way back over to the bed. He looked at her small, frail body, disgusted with himself. Sweet little Elly. What the hell was wrong with him? Could he have been so foxed he had not noticed it was her? Had he been so foxed he had hurt a woman?

He scanned her body and did not see any serious physical injuries, thank God. Only a bad bruise to her face and bruises on her arm. *I did that to her.* How could he have hurt someone he loved? What should he do? What if she was with child? What would his father or his uncle say?

Still shaking and trying to fight back tears, he straightened Elly up as best he could, taking care to wipe the blood away. He stoked the fire, and then threw her torn gown into the flames. He put another nightgown over her head and pulled the covers over her. She did not flinch when he touched her. He hoped she would not be able to remember what happened either—for her sake.

He made his way back to his room to wash, trying to fight the panic rising inside. He would have to tell his father. It might be better to just leave—or die. It might be better just to do everyone a favour and dispose of himself before his cousin did it for him. It was impossible to keep a duel a secret, no matter what. He did not want to be a coward, but he did not want to shame Elinor further. He knew Society did not give a jot for what a Duke's heir did. Frankly, that was probably why he had wrought the path of destruction he had. But this had crossed the line, even for him. He had not been this sober in years, and he deserved whatever punishment was given to him.

Nathaniel bathed himself quickly, even more disgusted after seeing the evidence of Elly's struggle against him. He was fairly well scratched and bruised all over, and his head was splitting with the worst pain he had ever felt. He was on the verge of loading the gun and taking it to Elinor. Would she feel better then? He packed a bag of his belongings and went to face his father.

The Duke of Loring was imposing, even in his shirt sleeves and without boots. He was still in his dressing room and gave Nathaniel a surprised look at seeing his son so early in the morning.

"Just coming in for the night?" his father asked with a disapproving eyebrow. The Duke was well aware of his son's activities and reputation in Town.

"No. I did not stay out last night," Nathaniel replied sombrely.

The Duke looked at his son and, noting his unusually bleak demeanour, dismissed his valet so they could speak alone.

"What is it you have to say? Have you finally been called out by an irate father or husband?"

"Not yet." Nathaniel could not look his father in the eye.

"I see. Pack your bags. We will leave after we break our fast," the Duke said angrily.

Nathaniel looked up in surprise. His father had never suggested running away from a problem.

"I have been considering this for some time as your behaviour has declined. I had already arranged to purchase your commission, should it become necessary. I believe that time has come. We will depart soon."

"There are some that I need to make amends with first," Nathaniel said, not expecting to leave quite so suddenly.

"Then write letters. I will see them delivered. See Hastings in on your way out." He was dismissed with the wave of his father's hand.

Nathaniel nodded. Arguing would do no good, and he had not the energy. He walked by Elly's room, but she was still asleep. He went to the library and tried to write out an apology, but no words made it to the paper. How did you write, *Forgive me for violating you?*

Perhaps it was better this way. He would force his way to the front lines in battle and let Fate take its course.

~*~

A few hours later, Nathaniel found himself on a packet to Portugal, bound for the Peninsular Campaign. He wondered, in a rare moment of rational thought, if he would live that long. His head was splitting; his body was shaking and sweating all over. He was immediately quarantined away from the rest of the soldiers.

"Lord Fairmont! Lord Fairmont! Can you hear me?" Someone shook Nathaniel's arm. He tried to force his eyes open, but when he did, the light seemed to cause horrible pains in his head, followed by uncontrollable bouts of retching.

"I am Dr. Craig. I am trying to help you," the doctor explained calmly.

Nathaniel managed a small nod between the violent tremors that wracked his body. He definitely needed a doctor.

"Have you been around anyone who was ill?"

He shook his head slightly.

"Do you have any idea what is wrong? Have you ever been like this before?"

"Too much." He paused for breath. "Whisky. Bad opium," he rasped.

Dr. Craig blew a frustrated breath through his lips. "How much whisky?"

"Bottles." His whole body was beginning to shake violently again. The doctor held him down until the seizing passed.

"This is not good. We are going to have to wean you off slowly. Otherwise, you will most surely die."

Nathaniel shook his head in vehement protest. "No more. Never again."

"You could die. It will get worse than this," the doctor said, adamant.

"Then let me die. It was my fault."

"What was your fault?" Dr. Craig tried to understand.

"I hurt her. I did that to her. I deserve this!" Lord Fairmont began jabbering deliriously. He continued talking nonsense and lost consciousness. Dr. Craig gave him some small amounts of laudanum and alcohol to help with the tremors and wean him off his dependence. Lord Fairmont was in bad condition and would likely die if he stopped taking those substances suddenly. When he was through the worst, they could discuss stopping for good.

This was Dr. Craig's first patient as an army physician, and how fortunate to get a spoiled, drunken lord, his first case on a long journey by sea. He had never treated anyone for acute withdrawal before, but he had studied this in school in Edinburgh. Studying and doing were two completely different animals. Watching this man suffer was akin to watching a mad dog.

Hallucinations, drenching sweats, veins pounding in his neck and shaking were just the beginning of what this young lord had to look forward to in order to conquer his demons—and more, from the sound of it.

AFTERWORD

Author's note: British spellings and grammar have been used in an effort to reflect what would have been done in the time period in which the novels are set. While I realize all words may not be exact, I hope you can appreciate the differences and effort made to be historically accurate while attempting to retain readability for the modern audience.

Thank you for reading *Seasons of Change*! I hope you enjoyed it. If you did, please help other readers find this book:

1. This ebook is lendable, so send it to a friend who you think might like it so they can discover me, too.
2. Help other people find this book by writing a review.
3. Sign up for my new releases at www.Elizabethjohnsauthor.com, so you can find out about the next book as soon as it's available.
4. Come like my Facebook page www.facebook.com/Elizabethjohnsauthor or follow on Twitter @Ejohnsauthor or feel free to write me at elizabethjohnsauthor@gmail.com

ALSO BY ELIZABETH JOHNS

Surrender the Past

Seasons of Change

Seeking Redemption

Shadows of Doubt

Second Dance

Through the Fire

Melting the Ice

With the Wind

Out of the Darkness

After the Rain

Ray of Light

First Impressions

ACKNOWLEDGMENTS

Many thanks to:

Wilette Youkey for being the role model, friend (the word doesn't do her justice) and mentor anybody would be lucky to have, not to mention talented author and design artist.

Wilette, Staci, Tammy, Judy, Melynda, Jill, and Dad for suffering through reading all of my rough drafts and providing invaluable advice.

My high school teachers, who "made" me read *Pride and Prejudice* and *Jurassic Park* as make-up work during convalescence one year.

Jill well, for just making me laugh and for "getting" me.

Holly for caring enough to notice something was wrong and for forcing me to talk about it.

Mom and Dad for raising me to believe I could do anything I put my mind to, and for being a constant source of love and support.

CJ for encouraging my dreams.

Nicholas and Ella for the smiles and hugs that make everything worth it.

Printed in the USA
CPSIA information can be obtained
at www.ICGtesting.com
LVHW092140310324
776020LV00001B/206